Drunk Log

A novel path to suicide

Books by Mark E. Scott

A Day in the Life series
Book 1: Drunk Log

Coming Soon!
A Day in the Life series
Book 2: First Date
Book 3: Free Will

For more information
visit: www.SpeakingVolumes.us

Drunk Log

A novel path to suicide

Mark E. Scott

SPEAKING VOLUMES, LLC
NAPLES, FLORIDA
2022

Drunk Log

Cover design by Hannah Linder

ISBN 978-1-64540-555-9

For Iris

Acknowledgments

I am eternally grateful to my agent, Nancy Rosenfeld, for believing, persevering, and making a lifelong dream a reality. I am equally grateful to my editor, David Tabatsky, of New York, my collaborator and fellow schemer. I owe a special debt to Kurt and Erica Mueller at Speaking Volumes, who were courageous enough to take a chance on me.

I have been lucky for much encouragement from those I care about. The list is long, but I'll start with my mother and father, Iris and Bob, who always kept life interesting. Also, I must thank Kristyn Brandenburg, astrophysicist, and hiking buddy. And there is Jim Debrosse, great friend, and inspiration, always willing to read me and offer advice.

I must include Sherri Scott, the mother of my children. I tortured her a page at a time, back in the day; Andy McClary, with whom I tried to write a novel when we were fifteen (the dream never dies); Nicole McCoubrey, always willing to listen and laugh, good or bad; Laura Peck, enthusiastic buyer of my words; Lisa Lickert and Linda Gravett, who helped set me on this path; Lisa Brandenberg, Charles Edmondson, Jeff Biehl, and Michelle Biehl, my first beta readers; Paul Gaitan, who quotes me at parties and lets me write in his basement; and, finally but not lastly, Jordan Simonson, writer, critic and confidant.

Finally, thank you to Dr. Liz Kraft, my technical expert. If I got anything wrong, blame her.

Chapter One

And So It Begins

Troy was sitting on his favorite uncle's lap, holding the steering wheel, pretending to drive, like any seven-year-old loves to do, when the truck hit. They were about to turn left, and Troy was laughing because his uncle kept tickling his neck. Jack had just taken a selfie of the two of them, smiling, freezing that moment in time. Neither one saw the truck coming as it struck the driver's side, carrying them forward until it skittered into a telephone pole.

> *4:00 p.m.*
> *Okay, I'm about to start my little experiment.*
> *I've been thinking about doing this for months and finally built up the courage to do it.*
> *I suppose, finally, I've had enough.*
> *This last year has been hell and I don't believe things will get better.*
> *I screwed up in the worst way I can imagine, and I'm paying for it.*
> *I don't think I'll ever stop paying for it, and that's probably as it should be.*
> *On that uplifting note, I'm reporting that my first bar is Liberty's.*
> *I'll see where the evening takes me after this.*
> *I'll do my best to record everything as accurately as possible.*

That way, anyone who reads it can make sense of what I'm about to do.

The results I leave to Posterity, from whom I also ask forgiveness.

In the world of bars and saloons, the time of day when Jack started writing might be classified as "half-time," too late for a day-drunk and too early for the bars to be busy.

Jack, sitting at the bar, nearly had the place to himself. His solitude was disturbed only by the bartender, going about her business, and two other patrons, sitting on a couch behind him. Jack thought he could feel them staring, but in reality, the couch-sitters were paying him little attention, writing as he was in the college-ruled notebook he had bought the previous day at a Dollar Store.

For Jack, the act of writing in his brand-new notebook left him feeling self-conscious and a bit ridiculous, and though he had ample experience sitting in bars, none of the time he'd spent on stools had ever included journaling, certainly not in public or, for that matter, at all.

Within just two minutes of writing his first words, he began questioning why he was doing it, even at such a familiar bar where he felt so comfortable. If there was any place he would feel comfortable writing in public, it would have been Liberty's, his second home. In spite of that, Jack began to feel like a self-conscious college freshman, desperate for attention but afraid to ask for it.

"What are you writing?" Aria asked, breaking Jack's concentration.

She placed the beer he had just ordered a respectful distance from the notebook, sensing its importance. Aria was used to seeing Jack in the bar, but not often alone, and never with a pen in his hand, at least not until it came time to pay the bill. It seemed odd to her, seeing him so engrossed, but she knew better than to ask too many questions.

"Oh, hey Aria, not much, just taking some notes. Thanks for the beer."

Jack moved the notebook another inch or two away from the beer, not unreasonably, fearing the glass might tip over on its pages, still mostly blank.

"No problem, Jack. Leave it open?"

Aria held up his credit card and gave it a little flourish.

"Yes, please."

Jack forced a smile, hoping she wouldn't ask any more questions.

"You got it."

Aria smiled and turned away from Jack, leaving him alone to stare down at the few words he had managed thus far to transplant from his brain to the paper. So far, he had written deliberately, one line at a time, perhaps to use up as many pages as possible, to see if he could fill up the entire notebook before the end of the night, before he killed himself.

He drank some beer and picked up his pen.

4:08

Okay, just started in on my first drink of the evening.

Probably a mistake to start with beer, now that I think about it.

You know—liquor before beer and all that.

In the end, it probably doesn't matter.

Hell, it may actually make this a better experiment.

I mean, I hope that the drunker I get, the more interesting it is for you, Posterity.

More interesting for me, too, no doubt.

Probably even write better as I get drunked up.

Hope so, anyway.

Never been much of writer, you should know that, I think.

Maybe my lack of ability will make you more inclined to over-look the occasional mistake.
Anyway, back to business . . .
It's a good beer, you know, the lager I'm drinking.
And, just so you know, Posterity, I don't like IPA's.
To me they taste like I imagine a dog fart would taste.
Never understood the IPA craze.
Just one man's opinion . . .

Autumn was on the wane and the early-evening sun lit the sidewalk just inches beyond the entrance to the bar. Jack tried to keep writing, looking to get on an early roll, but was distracted by people walking past the tall glass doors that formed the bar's front wall. Although he recognized a few of them, he was pleased to see that no one was choosing to enter.

He wasn't in the mood to be forced into conversation, preferring instead to sit alone with his thoughts, at least for the moment, at least for the beginning of this night. Meditating on the late daylight blazing into the bar, it occurred to Jack that he would likely become more gregarious as the evening progressed, as he always did, but at the moment he couldn't escape the desire for privacy and introspection. The irony of attempting to achieve privacy and introspection in a bar was not lost on him, but he rationalized the conflict by reminding himself that the bar was nearly empty, and that the inevitable sea of humanity had not yet intruded on his project.

Though his sense of being watched was initially misplaced, Jack was being observed, but the stealthy glances were not coming from the doorway or the couch behind him. The gazes were coming from across the bar, from Aria. She had been keeping an eye on him since he had walked in twenty minutes earlier. In fact, she had been keeping an eye on him for more than a year, since she started working at Liberty's.

Jack was a regular who lived in the building, and it hadn't taken long for Aria to become somewhat taken with him. They had even had a "moment" over the summer when he caught her staring at him, and, once he had consumed a sufficient amount of alcohol, he gently made mention of her attention.

"Are you staring at me?"

Jack was smiling, jovial as he pointed to his head with his left index finger.

"Is something weird happening with my hair?"

Jack had moved closer to the bar and was trying to speak "sotto voce," but the people sitting closest still heard him. Aria was embarrassed to get caught, but didn't deny what she had been doing. Instead, she told him that there was nothing wrong with his hair, and in a fit of daring, proclaimed that she actually liked his hair, and his eyes, black and blue, respectively.

"You do? Well . . . I like your eyes, too. And your hair."

Jack had been taken by surprise, which accounted for his somewhat less-than-smooth response. It was a busy, late Friday night and, in order to hear each other better, they leaned in from their respective sides of the bar. Finally, with their faces only intimate inches apart, Aria impulsively leaned in further, her reed-slim body stretching toward Jack, wordlessly eliminating what little space had remained between them until, ultimately, their lips were touching.

Both were surprised by what was happening, but both stayed in the kiss, at least until the sound of applause forced them to detach, each floating back to their side of the bar with embarrassed smiles.

The kiss had not been lost on the patrons pressed around them, well-wishers who clearly felt this singular event needed to be noted and celebrated. As quickly as she could, Aria went back to the business of bartending, leaving Jack standing on the other side of the bar, staring at her, looking confused even as he received back-slaps from well-meaning and well-lubricated onlookers.

Nothing came of the moment. It hadn't come up in any subsequent conversation. At all. Ever. Indeed, Aria had found a way to believe that Jack had forgotten it. She knew he'd had a lot to drink that night, more than enough to forget kissing the bartender. She also knew what had happened months before and felt she may have taken advantage of him on one of the rare nights he didn't seem preoccupied, when he seemed unburdened. With everything else going on with his life, she certainly didn't want to be included on his list of troubles. Besides, the customers had finally stopped ribbing her about the kiss. For the most part, anyway. In any case, as Jack pored over his notebook, seemingly lost in thought, their "moment" wasn't a can of worms she was ready to reopen.

4:12
Sometimes it's hard to sit in front of Aria, especially when it's pretty much just the two of us.
We kissed this past summer and it stuck with me.
It was a good kiss.
I mean . . . well, she's a good kisser.
I don't know how else to describe it.
We haven't talked about it, though.
I haven't brought it up and she hasn't either.
Maybe I should have asked her on a date that night.
I don't know, maybe I should say something now?
Oh my God, what a stupid idea.
What am I thinking?

Something like that would be cruel and stupid and she's too
good for me anyway.
Why would she tie herself to a sinking ship?
Why would I ask her to?
I want to say this about Aria—she still talks to me.
I know she knows what I did, and she still talks to me,
which is more than I can say for my sister-in-law, or even my
mother.

As Jack kept writing and worked his way through the lager, he forced himself not to look at Aria. Even though she kept stealing glances at him, he didn't catch her doing so. What he did notice, however, was that he had filled the first two pages of his notebook with actual words and sentences, now illuminated by the sunlight still flowing in through Liberty's windows.

Jack found the milestone of finishing two pages, though likely minor in the estimation of most, to be comforting, and the light glowing on his achievement was equally pleasing. It meant the night was young and Jack had plenty of time to drink and write. In fact, he was starting to enjoy the writing, which was unexpected.

In school he had never taken to it, preferring math and physics and the subjects that would propel him into a job as an engineer. It wasn't that he couldn't write. English was his native language, after all. It was just that he had found nothing but tedium in those classes, though he still managed to complete assignments, even if he had to convince or pay someone else to complete them for him.

But now, in the shadows of his local bar, he was finding it surprisingly comforting to release his thoughts from the prison of his brain and write the words in an order that would never change, at least as long as he didn't change them.

The written words, unlike his thoughts, were not fleeting and they didn't have to be recalled from memory should some circumstance warrant that effort. No. They were right there in front of him, staring back from a fresh notebook, and, for better or worse, that was the way Jack was determined to leave them. The fact that they were going to be a somewhat less-than-scientific accounting of how he had behaved during his last night of drinking was of no consequence. Certainly, he could have chosen a weightier topic to entice future readers. After all, Jack had considered other themes, like family or his work or even love, which could have aided him in the desired outcome, but none of them were as familiar or as easy to explore and discuss as the one he had landed on.

Drinking. He was good at it.

4:17
Almost finished with the beer, the first of the night.
For what it's worth, I'm experiencing what I'm used to experiencing after one beer.
Not much.
I've had enough first beers to know exactly how I'll feel, and tonight is like all the other times.
Relaxed and calm, ready for the next one.
It'll be the drinks coming later that will make this more interesting.
When I reach the point where things begin to mash together, where I've lost count, that's when the notes will really make a difference.
That's when they'll really get to the root of what I want to tell you, Posterity.

I figure I will try to have just one drink per bar, and there's more than enough bars in this neighborhood to make that a rule.

I'm going to break that rule already.

Maybe I'll follow it later, but it's my game so, Posterity, tell me: what's wrong with making the rules up as I go?

"Aria, could I get another, please?"

"Same kind?"

There were over twenty from which to choose, so Jack took a moment to study the list, written in chalk on the wall above the back of the bar.

"Hmmm. Yeah, I think so. Thanks, Aria."

Jack had considered using something other than alcohol in his experiment, perhaps one or more of a number of drugs, but felt there were a number of drawbacks with each of them.

He had enjoyed the effects of cocaine the few times he had tried it but feared those same, otherwise enjoyable effects would prevent him from stringing together coherent sentences. The memory of a six-hour, rambling conversation about politics with an attractive girl was enough to convince him to strike it from the list of potentials. He had little use for a drug, which made him waste that much time blathering about politics to anyone who would listen, especially someone to whom he desperately wanted to appear coherent and charming.

Methamphetamines were an option, but he was personally unfamiliar with their effects, so he could only rely on what he had read or seen on television. Besides a concern about the physical and mental incapacitation, which seemed to accompany the drug, at least as portrayed by the actors pretending to take it on TV, Jack felt that meth lacked a certain elegance. Perhaps this was, he mused, due to the prevalence of man-made ingredients in its production. Adding to the "cons" column was the fact that meth-heads always seemed to have bad teeth, something that offended his vanity.

Jack found the constellation of available drugs to be overwhelming. It had never occurred to him that there were so many options, legal and otherwise, until he forced himself to think about it. As a result, he quickly narrowed his search by eliminating whole categories, like over-the-counter drugs, prescription narcotics and almost all readily available street drugs. The most common reason for eliminating these options was insufficient personal experience, which was obviously necessary in order to gauge their potential effects.

Jack was convinced that if he was going to journal about a drug experience in real time, then an actual drug-induced coma (a la heroin) would be highly counterproductive. He had seen enough drugged-out zombies stumbling around the neighborhood to develop a healthy skepticism about their potential levels of literary production.

He even had to scratch marijuana from the list, a drug he knew enough about from personal experience. It wasn't so much that he feared the effects would keep him from writing; he just couldn't remember ever having a productive chat with a pothead, even when he was the pothead in question. This was mostly due to the fact that the answer to any question posed to a pothead is generally preceded by an annoying pause, during which the stoner is no doubt attempting to formulate a rational response, which Jack had rarely found to be forthcoming. To Jack, this behavior was supremely exasperating, especially in himself, so he scratched that option off the list.

After all, he told himself, he had been doing the necessary leg work on the effects of alcohol consumption for more than a decade, even longer, if one counts high school parties and the occasional pre-teen raid on his parents' liquor cabinet.

He knew he could control his intake in a way that would enable him to drink for hours, to consume enough to make the experiment meaningful. With that strategy in mind, he would take his time. After all, what's the point in getting hammered in three hours, only to spend the next few trapped in a round-robin of dry heaves, puke, and praying for it all to stop? Who hasn't read that story? Or lived it?

Though alcohol had been Jack's companion for years, it was not his master, a fact that added to the wisdom of his choice.

Feeling satisfied with his decision, Jack turned his attention back to the new page of the journal in an attempt to gather his thoughts and avoid being distracted by Aria. Looking down at the open pages of his notebook, now full of his thoughts, he realized that being pleased at having written so little was ridiculous. There were still ninety-eight blank pages left to fill. He would have to knuckle down if he was going to make any real progress.

4:23
I'm starting to think that Aria may be too much of a distraction to my experiment.
Maybe I should leave after this beer to go someplace where I haven't kissed anyone.
That shouldn't be too tall of an order.
I don't think there are more than a couple bars in the neighborhood where I've kissed anyone. Pretty sure none of those women actually worked in those bars.
I should be pretty safe almost anywhere but here, safe from this sort of thing, anyway.
I mean the Aria thing . . . hmm . . . the Aria thing.
I know I said something about this just a minute ago, Posterity.

While I'm still sober, I want to try to make sense of what she means to me, and WHY.

It wasn't just the kiss; it was everything that came AFTER the accident, including the kiss.

She always seemed to be in the bar when I needed her to be.

She always talked to me, which meant a lot.

She was always kind.

She was there when others weren't.

Without her, I probably would have done this months ago.

Not even Aria, or the thought of her, can stop me from it any longer.

It just hurts too much.

Jack put the pen down and stared at the last sentence, wondering what he was writing about. Why was this such a problem? He had kissed Aria months ago and tried to put it out of his head. Anything less would have been bad for her, and bad for him, too, at least according to his own temporary logic. Yet there he was, surreptitiously glancing at her.

Aria was standing at the end of the bar, pouring ice into a bin from a bucket. She didn't seem to notice him at all. Why was he making such a big deal about it? How could a kiss, until now essentially forgotten, or so he told himself, suddenly rise to such prominence?

He knew the answer to that question, but then again, maybe he didn't, depending on what he was willing to admit to himself.

While pondering this dilemma, Jack was joined at the bar, a bit rudely by his estimation, by a couple who had just come in. He didn't recognize them, which really wasn't the issue. The issue was, that for some inexplicable reason, these two people decided to sit right next to him—and his open notebook—at an otherwise empty bar.

The woman sat closest to Jack and started making what she likely considered a sly attempt to read what Jack had just written, at least until she noticed him staring at her, as if he were silently willing her to look the other way.

"What are you writing about?"

Jack barely shrugged.

"Do you mind me asking?"

Jack closed the notebook and picked it up off the bar.

"No, no, not at all. I was just about to move to the end of the bar anyway."

Jack's "answer" to a question that wasn't asked was received with a nervous smile. He almost felt guilty about picking up his things and moving to where Aria was pouring his beer. She had heard the exchange but pretended not to notice as she set Jack's beer in front of him.

But she felt a fury rising.

Chapter Two

Thank You Sir, May I Have Another

Jack was stunned by the crash, so much so that it took several minutes for him to realize what had just happened. As the initial shock faded, he could hear voices of people swarming around the car, but he couldn't discern their words. All he could discern was the strain of his body being crushed from all sides. All Jack could feel was Troy's body, trapped between his own and the steering wheel. He wasn't moving.

> *4:29*
> *Jeez! How rude was that?*
> *Some barfly just tried reading my journal without asking me if it was okay.*
> *What the hell?*
> *Can't believe she thought that was cool.*
> *I wonder if she reads over people's shoulders, too.*
> *I think I was nice, though, even when I moved away from her.*
> *Now, I'm sitting under the TV and the sound is kind of distracting.*
> *I think I got out of the chair wrong and now my hip hurts, the one I fractured in the crash.*
> *When will this damn thing ever be right again?*
> *Ha! Probably never, considering.*
> *That's fine, I don't mind the reminder.*
> *It won't matter soon, anyway.*

Aria watched Jack limp ever so slightly to a seat at the end of the bar and start scribbling in his notebook. She grabbed the remote to lower the volume on the TV and felt an anger rising in her stomach and chest. She wanted nothing more than to jump across the bar and tackle the bitch who was trying to read Jack's notebook without his permission.

Despite her ire, Aria managed to take the couple's drink order with a smile on her face while simultaneously calculating her chances of spitting in the woman's drink without being detected. She decided that it was too disgusting and opted instead to accidentally spill some wine on the girl's purse.

"Oops! Sorry about that!"

Aria received a stern frown for her faux apology.

Jack's head was buried in his log so he didn't notice the exchange, but he would have appreciated Aria even more because of it. His head remained down even after he was done writing. This allowed him a moment to meditate, to temper his anger and allow the stabbing fire in his hip to subside before looking up to see a new beer sitting in front of him.

He had grown somewhat used to the constant flow of pain, and even forgot about it sometimes. In a way, he was happy to be reminded of it, especially when it stabbed at him the way it was now.

4:30

Just got my second beer.

It usually doesn't take me this long to finish one beer, but it's early.

I'm already wondering if I can keep up the writing all night.

What about when I really start feeling the effects of the alcohol?

15

I'm not anywhere near that yet; it'll take a couple more.
You'll forgive me, Posterity, if this gets a little boring at
times.
I've never been good at writing, and this is kind of a
pressure situation.
I'm liable to write some crap in here just to flesh it out a
little, just like I did in high school.

Jack held his pen in one hand and the beer in the other. He stared at his notebook, took a deep breath and then lifted his head away from the page just long enough to exhale slowly and take a long slug from the glass Aria had set in front him. As soon as it settled inside him, he turned his attention back to the log and began writing again.

4:32
This may sound crazy, but sometimes I wish the pain in my
hip and leg was worse than it is.
I wish I could feel it all the time, so I had something
nagging me to never forget.
It would mean the karmic wheel is still turning and I'm
getting what I deserve.
For a long time, I thought Charlie would just stop talking to
me, like Sarah did.
I don't know why he didn't, and I wouldn't have blamed
him.
Early on, after the funeral, we all sort of went into hiding, I
think.
I think we were avoiding what happened, hiding from each
other, or at least trying to.
Sarah, mostly.

I wanted to hide from everything and everybody.
Couldn't stand the thought of being around my brother and
sister-in-law.
I took their boy away.
They could have killed me, and I would have understood.

Jack put the pen down abruptly, not entirely sure of why he wrote those last few sentences or from what part of him they came. To the best of his knowledge, he had never actually said those things before, not to himself and certainly not to anyone else. He was surprised the thoughts popped out of him so easily. They came unexpectedly, to a degree that frightened him. He put the pen down before it could write any more unsolicited words on the page. It seemed to have gained a certain independence, free of Jack's intentions, and though it was now safely lying on the bar, he couldn't take his eyes off of it.

"Everything good?"

Aria had moved back to Jack's end of the bar after serving the bitch and the bitch's boyfriend. She was determined to run cover for Jack as long as he needed it.

Aria's voice broke the pen's hold on Jack's attention.

"Oh, yeah, thanks, Aria. Everything's great."

"Let me know if you need anything."

Like a baseball bat, she thought.

When Aria turned away, it occurred to Jack that the beer might be affecting him more than he expected, and that this reaction might explain what just happened with the log. He pondered that possibility for just a moment before dismissing it.

One beer, even a strong one, couldn't affect him that drastically. He had never been a "gusher," the guy that tells all his friends how much he loves them after he's had a few too many. For the most part, Jack's friends were able to discern his level of drunkenness only by subtle changes in his behavior. Maybe he laughed a little louder than usual, or maybe it was a little harder to get his attention. But only those in the know had a chance of reading those signals. If you existed outside of Jack's close circle of friends, or had not learned to pay attention, you might assume that alcohol didn't affect him at all, at least not until the next morning, when there might be hell to pay.

Jack recognized the honesty of his writing as aberrant, and while he was nearly always honest with others, he avoided being that honest with himself as much as possible. He would have to dig a little deeper to figure out what was going on with his disobedient pen.

By now, nearly all the bar stools were full, but Aria was still standing a couple feet away from Jack with her arms folded. She had taken care of everyone wanting service and had assumed a relaxed posture that broadcast her level of control over all things bar related.

Jack still didn't recognize anyone and was happy he didn't. He knew his desire to remain anonymous for the entirety of the experiment was unrealistic, given the number of people in the neighborhood he knew and that knew him.

He would enjoy the luxury while he could. For the moment, at least, he was being left alone, apart from the glances, which he thought were aimed at him but were really directed to the television hovering a couple feet over his head. He figured he was hiding in plain sight, his identity only known to the bartender, who appeared to have assumed the role of an accomplice.

4:35
I suppose I'm going to have to get used to having people around me while I write this log.
It is Friday, after all.

*I guess I could have done this on a Monday, but I doubt I
could find an empty bar even then.*
*I've been here on Monday nights when there were twenty or
thirty people.*
*I'm just going to have to suck it up and do the research, no
matter who's staring me down.*

As Jack paused and stared at the last sentence, he let go a short laugh
and hoped no one noticed. He didn't want to look like the neighborhood
kook, talking to himself and laughing at his own jokes.

4:37
Now that's funny.
Research.
Hilarious.
*Like this is the first time I've ever done "research" at a
bar.*
*You should know, Posterity, that I've spent thousands of
dollars on "research" and only rarely regretted it, and then
only for a couple of hours.*
Maybe for a day but never more than that.
*I've thoroughly enjoyed 99 percent of my research, but I
just never called it that.*
Maybe I should have.
*Maybe I could have gotten a discount if I told all those
bartenders I was writing a story about the effects of
alcohol.*
*And to the point, which I'm getting away from again, I'm
already halfway through my second beer and, other than
my little outburst on the previous page, it appears I'm still*

pretty sober.

Actually, I just checked out the glass and I'm not quite halfway done.

Under normal circumstances, when I'm not trying to record my "feelings,"

I would be on my third or fourth by now, or at least my third.

By the way, I'd go back and fix the sentence where I said I was halfway done but I've decided to not make any additions or deletions.

Posterity, I'll let you do that for me.

I don't know, maybe the beer is having some effect.

I keep talking to Posterity as if it's a person.

That's just silly.

Jack smiled at his attempt at humor and took a sip of his beer. The sun continued to descend behind him, behind the television floating over his head and in front of Aria, who was again facing his way, taking a drink order from two newcomers standing on Jack's side of the bar. He didn't notice them until he put his pen down and closed the notebook to protect the words from prying eyes. The girl from the other end of the bar had done him the favor of teaching him a lesson he wouldn't forget for the rest of the evening. Whatever he wrote was not meant to be read tonight. It was for later. For Posterity.

Still, he found their intrusion annoying even if they couldn't read the log, and despite the fact that he knew better. Personal space at a busy bar is a luxury. Despite the jostling, for which he received a semi-sincere "Sorry, dude," Jack understood that one has to make room for those behind him, wanting to order. Basic bar etiquette. Jack took a couple of deep breaths and fought the desire to spread his elbows wider.

Aria, however, was still feeling protective.

"Hey guys," she said, as she handed two beers across the bar. "There's a couple open seats at the other end if you feel like grabbing some wood."

Jack mouthed "thanks" to Aria as the new patrons exited the boundaries of Jack's self-declared personal space. Aria gave him a little nod and a smile and glanced down to check his beer before deciding he wasn't ready for another.

> *4:45*
> *I'm going to have to get over myself.*
> *Just so you know, Posterity, a couple guys were just trying*
> *to get drinks and I got pissy because one of them*
> *accidentally bumped into me.*
> *He even apologized.*
> *I feel like a douchebag.*
> *Aria got them to move, and I figured she did it for me,*
> *which I thought was sweet.*
> *If I was smart, I'd tell her what I'm doing and see if she*
> *could run interference for me all night.*
> *But I'm not smart.*
> *She has to work anyway.*
> *She can't babysit ME all night.*

Though Jack was alone and intended to be for the duration of his experiment, part of him had an inkling that he didn't really want to be—alone. The part of him that was indulging in that inkling wasn't the part that was in charge of his behavior, and so Jack was kept in the dark, at least for the moment, by one of his own inner voices.

The inkling, though, was growing into an idea, and would eventually evolve into a full-grown belief, but that would happen later, when it was too late for him to ask Aria to babysit for him, or so it seemed. For now, the inkling was still tiny. It was too small to be heard and needed time to grow if it was going to have any effect on Jack, who was busy pouring beer on it, which wasn't necessarily a bad thing. Historically, small ideas tended to grow when liberally doused with alcohol, at least for Jack.

He was making a point to stare blankly at the wall beyond Aria, past the other end of the bar. That way, she wouldn't think he was staring at her, but also because he needed time to ponder his next move and felt it was somehow better to stare across the bar at a wall than directly down at his notebook. Jack figured that staring at the notebook might draw more attention to its' existence, more attention than just staring at a blank wall.

Jack was quite a logical person.

For all the thought Jack put into the concept of the log, he failed to put much at all into the actual mechanics of the evening he had devised. He knew he would drink all night, but hadn't mapped it out, at least not beyond where he was going to start his experiment. In the moment, he thought he should probably move on to the next bar, but that begged the question of which one, something he still had to figure out.

Oddly enough, however, the blank staring was having a serendipitous effect on Jack and his pondering. He knew that was true because he realized he had identified a hole in his plan and was consciously devising a fix for it, even though it wasn't a problem that would require an astrophysicist to fix. His first choice was simple enough: choose to stay or choose to go.

He stared past Aria, weighing the potential merits of each course of action. And then he picked up his pen again.

4:50
Should I stay or should I go?
I know, I know. Stealing from The Clash, but I don't think they'll mind.
They'll never read this anyway, but I have to decide.
There's something so beautifully simple about staying put here all night, at least until it's actually time to go.
It's a big enough bar to move around in, I mean, at least if I want to change seats or stare at a different wall. But going somewhere else has a nice sound to it.
What if I want to listen to live music before the end of the evening?
For that, I have to go up the street.
I guess the bottom line is, I don't have to decide right now, which I suppose is a decision in itself, so I guess I'm deciding to stay, at least for now . . . uh huh . . . at least for now.

The act of making the decision, even in a half-assed, roundabout way, pleased Jack. He rewarded himself by drinking half of what was left in his glass. Making the decision felt so good he decided he was going to go ahead and make a few more, the first being what his next drink would be.

This decision wasn't going to be as easy or coincidental as the last one, mostly because during the last decade or so, or mostly since getting out of college and getting a paying job, Jack was quick to realize that he enjoyed the variety of ways alcohol could be mixed and served. So, while he truly loved beer, he also loved Manhattans, Black Russians, Moscow Mules, and Scotch, and any number of concoctions he didn't always have time to try. To help with the decision process, he resumed staring at the wall past Aria.

Of course, she had taken notice of Jack's wall-staring posture. When it came to what was going on at or near the bar, Aria noticed nearly everything. She deduced correctly that Jack was attempting to work out some problems, though she didn't fathom the complexity, or lack thereof, of the current problem at hand. She also rightly assumed that he was doing his best not to stare at her, or at anyone in particular. Instead, he fixed his gaze carefully so as not to annoy anyone or make them uncomfortable, including her. She felt the exercise was ridiculous and almost laughed out loud. Finally, she had enough.

"Hey, Jack."

She walked over, carrying a bar towel, which she used to wipe the area of the bar directly in front of his notebook.

"Are you thinking about another drink?"

Aria's perception startled him.

"Um, yes, as a matter of fact. Any suggestions?'

The question was all the more felicitous due to the fact that the bartenders at Liberty's knew what he liked. This was important since the beer selection changed regularly, and Jack had to rely on their depth of knowledge to make sure his experience was a good one. There were too many to choose from and the information on the chalkboard was not always displayed adequately enough to relay sufficient information about the flavor and nuance of every beer listed. That was the bartender's job.

"How about a Manhattan? Rye Manhattan?"

"Always a good choice, but are you sure you don't want another beer?"

Aria subscribed to the "beer before liquor, never sicker" school of thought, and this was her gentle attempt to ward Jack away from potential disaster, albeit a slow-moving one.

Jack's brow furrowed for an instant as the inevitable flash of doubt about his drink choice took momentary control over his facial expression.

"No, but thanks, Aria. I'll have the Rye Manhattan."

"You got it."

Jack watched her as she made the drink. She was not a slave to measurement and seemed to rely more on experience and instinct. The sun was finally beginning to set through the window behind Jack, casting an orange glow on the white, sleeveless shirt Aria had donned for her shift. Had it not lacked sleeves it could have been worn with a tuxedo. He had never seen her in that particular shirt, at least not that he could recall, and caught himself staring at her again.

The wall beyond Aria, covered with bottles of wine for sale, the same space he had been staring at, was now blocked by early evening drinkers so he could no longer stare at it without feeling he was staring at a stranger. Abandoning the wall, he went ahead and polished off the remainder of his beer just as Aria set the Manhattan in front of him.

"Thanks, Aria."

"My pleasure, Jack. I hope you like it."

"I will."

The crowd seemed to be growing exponentially as the bar filled up with the after-work-and-before-dinner crowd, made up of a combination of regulars and others just exploring the neighborhood. Nearly every establishment was within four or five blocks of each other, so people could walk to their dinner destinations, and perhaps come back later.

Jack did not have any dinner plans. In fact, he planned to not eat anything more than the peanut butter sandwich and corn chips he had consumed before leaving his condo and walking around his building to the front door of Liberty's. After all, food would slow down the effects of the alcohol and get in the way of his experiment. He would do his best not to let anything get in the way of that and its inevitable climax.

Chapter Three

Three and Out

A noisome concoction of gasoline, oil and blood-filled Jack's nostrils, and his abject fear was shared by those outside the mangled heap of metal, which just two minutes ago appeared to be a Toyota Camry. The blood was mostly his. Jack struggled to find his voice, to separate it from those trying to get his attention outside the compressed pile of steel, which had him trapped inside. Finally, it came, a single word that meant everything, the only one that mattered. It emerged quietly at first, like a whisper. "Troy?" He realized he could move his right hand just enough to touch the boy's leg. Enveloped by fear, the word came out in a scream. "TROY!"

5:05
I think I have to leave, not that I really want to, but I have to.
It would be good to get around the neighborhood tonight, sort of a tour, or a final lap.
This would be good for the experiment.
Besides, I need to spread the wealth around, sprinkle myself, here and there.
I can always come back if people start bugging me too much.
Liberty's is probably the safest place for that, but I'm not sure that's exactly what I want.
I think I need to get around so I might even go someplace I've never been before.
Okay, Posterity, that was a joke.

I've been everywhere in Over the Rhine.

More and more patrons kept piling in, until their collective hum made one conversation indistinguishable from another. Jack found the white noise comforting and he allowed himself to bathe in it as he took a sip of the Manhattan Aria had made for him. The drink was perfect, of course. Aria was a maker of perfect Manhattans. But it was made even more sublime because it was Jack's third drink, and he was beginning to feel the felicity he was used to feeling with drink number three.

The self-consciousness, which had been plaguing him since his arrival in the bar was being replaced with a simple joy, the kind of warmth that makes a seat feel more comfortable than it really is, which can cause people to become more interesting than they really are.

Indeed, it was an excellent Manhattan.

5:06
What to do?
What to do?
What to do?
This may be the best drink I've ever had.
I may not require any further research to declare this a
fact.
Oh Posterity, can't you take a joke?

Jack may or may not have been ready to write more in this particular log entry, but a slap on his back forced a temporary hold on his written reverie. He would have to wait to write more until the conclusion of this imminent encounter.

The slap came from Fireman Jack, who Jack had known since moving onto Main Street. Fireman Jack was just one of many Jacks in the "hood," who lived about a block from where Liberty's and Engineer

Jack were located. Interesting to some, between his building and the bar there were three more Jacks, not including the two currently at the bar. There were the Gay Jacks, who lived three buildings south of Liberty's, and a bonus Fireman Jack, who lived in the building next to the Gay Jacks. Engineer Jack wasn't sure how many total Jacks there actually were in OTR, but he believed whole-heartedly that five Jacks living within one block of each other was statistically improbable.

At times, being neither gay nor a fireman left him feeling like he was being kept out of an otherwise informal club, despite the fact that none of the other Jacks had ever made him feel unwelcome for not being a member of either group.

"Hey, Jack."

Fireman Jack was standing behind Jack, the log, and his Manhattan, towering over them all. At six feet seven inches, he was nearly a head taller than Engineer Jack and the height differential was maximized by the fact that Engineer Jack was sitting on a stool.

"How are you feeling?"

Jack closed the log as discreetly as he could, hoping the notebook would remain unnoticed, given the elevation of Fireman Jack's standing line-of-sight.

"Hi, Jack. I'm good. Good. Where's Lucy?"

"She's on her way. She's just finishing up some things at work."

Lucy was Fireman Jack's girlfriend and roommate. She managed a bar just a couple blocks away.

"Can I buy you a drink?"

"Oh . . . no, thanks, Jack. I just got this one."

Engineer Jack waved his left-hand toward the brand-new Manhattan sitting next to his notebook on the copper bar, as if he were presenting it as a prize on a game show.

"Cool. Looks good."

29

Fireman Jack referred to the Manhattan before turning his glance to the Drunk Log.

"What you got going there?"

Despite the increased bar traffic, Aria had been keeping an eye on the two Jacks. She would never shoo Fireman Jack away as she would nearly anyone else, but she wasn't about to give him complete access to Engineer Jack, either, especially while he was in such an obvious funk. She intervened only when she saw Fireman Jack point to the notebook, walking to the end of the bar and getting the Jacks' attention.

"I'm sorry guys, let me get this out of your way."

Aria smiled while deftly sliding the notebook off the bar and hiding it on the shelf directly below the Manhattan.

"I can't believe I left that out where Jack could spill his drink on it!"

She looked at Engineer Jack, her Jack, trying to gauge his reaction to what she had just done, and was relieved to see him mouth the words "Thank you" before turning his attention back to Fireman Jack.

Beneath the bar, with her free hand, Aria opened the drunk log to page one as she stared across the bar at the Jacks. Though a tinge of guilt crept into her curiosity, she couldn't resist the opportunity to find out what he had been writing, even if she wasn't quite sure when she'd have the opportunity to read it.

Her behavior was impulsive, and she had no plan, so for the moment she just left the log safely tucked under the bar, where no one but her could see it. She knew she'd have to figure it out quickly, however, given the fact that her Jack might ask for it back at any moment. She was saved from this particular ethical dilemma by another distraction. While she was toying with the notebook, Lucy pushed her way through the crowd to Fireman Jack's side.

"Hi, Luce."

"Hey, Aria. Hi Jack."

Lucy wrapped her boyfriend's arm around her shoulders. She was nearly a foot-and-a-half shorter and weighed little more than a hundred pounds. If the size difference caused them any concern it wasn't at all apparent.

"Can I get a number 9?"

While Lucy ordered a beer from the numbered list on the chalkboard, Jack was riding the jagged edge of an anxiety attack. A moment ago, Aria's little trick with the notebook had pleased him, but now he felt ill at ease. Holding his ground, at least for the moment, he forced himself to take deep breaths, just as he had learned to do in physical therapy.

This calming technique came in handy as he waited for Aria to finish pouring Lucy's beer, and he managed to sit motionless until the glass was full. He wasn't sure how he was going to go about getting the notebook back without revealing its true ownership, but the task was made easier when, after receiving her beer, Lucy suggested she and Fireman Jack move away from the bar and take seats on the couch by the far wall.

As soon as their view of him was obscured, Jack got Aria's attention.

"Do you want it back?"

Aria had read his mind again.

"Yeah, I do. Can you grab it for me?"

"Sure, but aren't you worried about them?"

Aria motioned toward Fireman Jack and Lucy while maintaining eye contact with Jack.

"No. I mean . . . it's okay. They're sitting over there and won't see it. I'll stash it if they start walking around or notice it again."

Jack thought for a moment.

"You know what. Can you hold on to it for a couple minutes? I have to use the restroom."

"No problem. I'll watch your drink for you."

31

Aria was washing glasses and waited until Jack disappeared around the corner before opening the notebook with her still-wet hands. She read as fast as she could. Jack printed his words like an elementary school kid, but it was still somewhat sloppy, so she slowed her pace through the prose.

His comments on the girl who interrupted his writing made her smile, and she felt heartsick when he talked about his brother and sister-in-law. But it was Jack's ruminations on their kiss and the way he felt around her, which made her smile again.

Aria managed to get through several pages before stopping from fear of getting caught. She wasn't so much worried about Jack being angry as she was about hurting him. She felt guilty, too. It occurred to her that she was no better than the rude bitch whose purse she had spilled wine on, but she was able to dismiss that thought soon enough.

Aria's interest in Jack was no passing fancy or a flighty interest expressed to some random stranger, waiting for a drink. She knew that with every word she read.

When Jack came back, she was pouring a beer, happy to know that her position at the taps was a clear indication of her industriousness, a signal that nothing untoward had happened in Jack's absence. Such a hard-working individual would never allow herself to be distracted by a notebook, and certainly wouldn't have time to read it, even if its owner was absent long enough to take a peek. Clearly, she was too busy for that sort of thing.

Jack fidgeted at the end of bar, shifting his weight from one leg to the other, staring at Aria, willing her to finish her task so she could give pass him the log. It worked. Without a word, she glided toward him, grabbed the log from under the counter, and handed it over.

"Thanks, Aria."

The log felt good in his hand.

"Anything for you, Jack."

Aria tried to sound flippant and matter of fact, but she heard neither of those qualities in her voice. Was it guilt? She turned on her heel as her face began to flush.

Jack, back in his spot but surrounded by bustling drinkers, pulled the pen from the wire spine and opened the log, noting the wet spots that appeared on several pages.

5:12

I feel like I was being anti-social with Fireman Jack and Lucy. Maybe I drove them away, or maybe they just wanted to be alone on the Big Comfy Couch.

I'm kinda glad. I always feel small around Jack, and I'm not small.

I'm six feet tall, damnit, at least on most days.

He's just so big.

I think he could take Lucy and swing her around over his head for fun.

Maybe he does, and that's what they do for fun when nobody else is around.

I'm not going to judge.

Jack took a swig of the Manhattan and looked around to make sure that Fireman Jack and Lucy couldn't see what he was doing. In a mostly ridiculous attempt to hide that he was writing in a bar, he hunched over the notebook like it was the first plate of food he'd eaten in a week. Somehow, it didn't occur to him that everyone standing inches away could see what he was doing, or that his posture might draw attention to the fact that something weird was going on at his end of the bar. But the others were preoccupied with their own socializing, and those milling about in close proximity showed little or no interest in the hunchback writing in a notebook.

5:13
I wonder if Aria was reading this while I was in the bathroom.
She might have just spilled some water on it while it was under the bar.
The spots were on the pages.
I'm not going to ask her.
Don't want to embarrass her, and if she didn't read it, I just look like an ass.

Jack fiddled with his pen and looked back through the pages he'd filled so far, still wondering if Aria could have possibly scanned them all while he was in the bathroom. As he mused on that, he took another sip of the Manhattan.

5:14
I mean, damn, this is the best Manhattan I've ever had.
It's almost like I'm blind or deaf, and because of that my other senses are heightened.
That makes this drink better than any drink I've ever had.

The space around Jack was filling up fast. What had been a low hum had evolved into a steady drone of loud voices competing to be heard. He looked up and watched Aria working the crowd from behind the bar. She was alone, but most of the patrons made her job easier by drinking either beer or wine, both readily available from taps jutting out from the wall behind her. Multiple orders for mixed drinks, like Jack's, would have impacted her efficiency. The grace she had developed from thousands of hours of dance class was apparent as she nearly floated from one end of the bar to the other, her auburn hair lightly bouncing from side to side as she moved this way and that. Jack observed her and his heart sank.

5:16
I wonder if she knows all the details.
Aria.
I've never asked her, and she's never asked me, either.
I wonder how she would feel if she knew the whole story.
Would she hate me, like Sarah does?
Would she spit in my drink?
Would she even serve me?
But you know what, Posterity?
I don't even want to think about this shit right now.
Why does it keep bleeding in?
Is it the pen?
Do all Bic pens have this power?
Now, just think about that.
What if all Bic pens were magic and made people write things they didn't want to write?
That sounds like a big problem to me.
I mean, if all you had to do to get to the truth was hand a piece of paper and a Bic pen to someone, it would change the world.
But maybe I'm overreaching.

Jack downed a little more of the Manhattan and watched Aria. Her back was to him so she wouldn't catch him staring again. And he was staring. He couldn't take his eyes off the ivy vine tattoo growing from her shoulder, down her left bicep, to her elbow. It followed the slender contours of her arm. He found it mystifying. He took a moment before picking up the pen.

5:20
I'm tired.
That's all I am anymore.
I'm tired of the pain that doesn't ever seem to go away.
Tired of doctor's appointments.
Tired of feeling guilty and having nightmares.
I don't even try to see Charlie anymore.
All I want to do whenever I'm around him is apologize.
I have to fight it.
Saying sorry, I mean, because all it does is make him feel bad again.
It makes him remember, too, not that he can ever forget.
Not that any of us can.
I begged him again, not long ago.
I begged him and Sarah to forgive me.
Couldn't help myself.
I'm tired of being alone.

Jack wasn't sure if he had holstered the pen into the wire binding of his own free will or if the pen had decided it was done writing, at least for the moment. He thought it could be possible that the Bic didn't like what he was writing. Maybe he sounded too whiny, and it just wasn't that kind of pen. Regardless, he took it as a sign and instead of pulling it back out, he allowed his gaze to drift around the room.

All around him were couples and groups. Unsurprisingly, Jack couldn't identify anyone else hovering over a notebook, writing about their feelings in the middle of a busy saloon. On top of that, he noticed that no one else was alone. No one at all. He couldn't even locate anyone who appeared to be waiting for someone else. Nope.

Jack was the only one lacking an "other," and as that little epiphany hit him, he caught Aria looking his way, checking up on him again. Being under her watchful eye comforted him, but he realized he had to get his ass out of the chair and move around. Miniscule though it was, that realization had enough power to make him get up and move, and a moment later he was making his way across the wooden floor, Manhattan held aloft, above the pulsing throng of couples and groups.

"Mind if I hang out with you guys?"

Fireman Jack and Lucy smiled and slid to the right, making room for him on the couch next to Lucy. He did not have his log. Somehow, he had forgotten it in his rush to move about. Glancing over at the bar, he caught Aria grabbing it and sliding it back into its hidey-hole, below the copper bar. Feeling secure, he sat down next to Lucy, placing the remainder of his Manhattan on the coffee table in front of them.

"So, Lucy, how's the bar business?"

Jack was still feeling the joy generated by the Manhattan, as well as the secondary effect of sociability so common to nearly everyone working on their third drink.

"It's fine, Jack. Busy, which is good. How come I never see you over there?"

The bar Lucy managed was four blocks away from Liberty's. It was a nice enough place, but four blocks could be a lot of distance to overcome, considering the plethora of drinking establishments within a stone's throw of Jack's home.

"I don't know, Luce. I try to get over there but always end up at some other place."

"Jeez, Jack. I see you walking past the place on your way home from work. You can't just stop in?"

Lucy was sporting a smile with a touch of derision.

While Jack was defending his leisure-time choices to Lucy, another bartender came by to give Aria a break, which she gratefully accepted. Sensing an opportunity, she grabbed Jack's notebook, and with as little fanfare as possible, spirited it from the bar and into the bathroom, where she planned to finish reading what Jack had written.

She felt guilty again, of course, but rationalized that the invasion of privacy was necessary, even though she couldn't quite put her finger on why that was true. Taking the log to the bathroom made her feel like she was killing two birds with one stone, which in turn made her feel simultaneously efficient and helpful. Besides, she told herself, she would be back at the bar before Jack even noticed her absence.

Seated on the cool toilet seat, she located the pages she hadn't yet read and dug in, blushing when she saw that Jack already suspected she may be reading his journal. She laughed at his treatise on the awful power that might be contained in an otherwise humble Bic pen.

The last entry, however, took her breath away, and she felt ashamed. Her selfishness had brought her to this moment, hiding in a bar bathroom reading a friend's deeply personal thoughts. She had no right to read it. Jack wasn't exposing himself to her, in particular. Not at all. She closed the notebook, wound her way back behind the bar, and put it quickly back on the shelf as if it were burning her hand. She promised herself she would not do that to Jack again.

Fireman Jack and Lucy repeatedly ignored Jack for a few seconds at a time in order to trade a look or a kiss or a few quiet words, meant only for each other. Jack took those occasions to look around the bar, at anything, as long as he didn't have to watch the happy couple.

He could do nothing else. Staring at them in their moments of intimacy would have been rude and just made him uncomfortable. Fireman Jack and Lucy did not give Jack much time to stare around the bar, however. Instead, they reeled him back into conversation as soon as they finished whatever cozy exchange they were sharing.

"What's going on over there?"

Fireman Jack waved his hand in the general direction of Jack's most recent stare.

"Not much. Not much at all, really."

Jack brought his gaze back around to his couch mates and downed the last drink of his Manhattan, allowing the rye and vermouth to roll around on his tongue, savoring the final sweetness and slight burn of it before swallowing.

Lucy stood up when Jack set the empty glass on the coffee table.

"You ready for another?"

Jack stood up, too.

"Thanks, Luce, but I think I'm going to head out, see what I can see."

"Where are you headed?"

"Not sure. Maybe MOTR. Maybe Dirty Helen's. We'll see."

Lucy wrapped her arms around him.

"Let us know where you end up. Maybe we'll meet you over there."

"You bet."

Jack hugged Lucy back, but he had no intention of letting them know where he was going. That could have been because he wanted to be alone with his thoughts and his notebook. Or it could have been because he didn't want to involve them in his experiment any more than he had already. He wasn't sure why and didn't take time to figure it out. His burning desire at the moment was to retrieve the log and disappear.

He stood at the bar and waited for Aria to realize he was there. She knew exactly where he was, of course, but was forcing herself not to drop everything she was doing every time she thought he needed something. Her task complete, she smiled at Jack and tried not to look guilty as she reunited him with his notebook, the pen still perfectly trapped in the wire rings.

"Thanks, Aria."

Jack was disappointed that their hands didn't touch when he took the log from her.

"Heading out?"

"Uh, yeah. You know, kinda see what I can see."

To Jack the words, now repeated, sounded stupid and contrived. He wished he hadn't said them, especially to Aria.

"Okay, well, have fun. Maybe I'll see you later?"

Aria thought she heard a trace of yearning in her voice and wondered if Jack heard it, too. She kept talking.

"You know, Jack, if you don't have anything else to do. I'll probably be around here. I mean, maybe."

Now she was just babbling. She closed her mouth.

"Yes, of course. Maybe. Thanks again, Aria."

Jack wanted to leave and didn't want to leave and so he turned toward the door while his will was still strong enough to do so. It was only three steps to the sidewalk, but instead of walking out he turned and took the log to the bathroom.

Chapter Four

A Walk in the Park

Jack couldn't stop screaming the boy's name. Panic overwhelmed every one of his senses and he kept screaming, even as part of his brain told him to stop. Some part of him, some deep, unreasonable part, hoped if he screamed loud enough the boy would wake up. He knew it was a lie, but he kept screaming anyway. He couldn't stop. The screams rattled the interior of the ruined Camry, bouncing, careening off the deflated airbags, collapsing windows, and cracked molding. By now four bystanders were calling 911 and the driver of the dump truck, a man named Robert McMullen, was sitting on the curb, sobbing.

5:31

What the fuck am I doing in this bathroom?

Am I afraid to leave? Am I actually afraid to leave this bar?

Okay, Posterity, in case you haven't figured it out, right now I'm sitting on the toilet in the bathroom. I'm not pooping or anything. Just sitting.

I was going to leave and go somewhere else, but my feet carried me in here.

It was an out of body experience, but not the good kind.

I mean, I ended up in the bathroom, pants up, sitting on the toilet seat cover.

What kind of shitty out of body experience is that? Shouldn't I be in bed next to some random hot girl I just met in the bar, or on the street, or at work?

*Instead I'm sitting here, worried about toilet paper sticking to
my shoes.*
I knew I should have studied Buddhism harder.
That might have helped me understand what I'm doing now.
*Anyway, I need to get out of here but this IS pretty private. I
could get a lot of writing done here.*
Nope—no, no no.
*I'm not going to let my mind trick me into camping out in a bar
restroom.*
I've got to go, Posterity.
Time to bend my body to my mind's will.

Jack stood up and set the notebook on the edge of the sink so he
could use both hands to pull his pants up and cinch his belt. Not surprisingly, the edge of the sink was wet, allowing the cardboard backing of
the binder to absorb some of the water, creating a slashing, wet scar.
Jack thought the scar appropriate. After all, there was nothing he could
do about it now, and with the accumulating water stains, the notebook
was beginning to earn a little character. Until that moment, the notebook
was perhaps a little too pristine and definitely not in keeping with how
Jack had been feeling about his own existence. Perhaps, since he was
writing about himself, the appearance of the notebook, and not just the
words, should reflect his personal zeitgeist. It also occurred to him to
look up the word "zeitgeist" on his phone before he tried to use it in a
sentence. He didn't want Posterity to think him an idiot.

When Jack opened the bathroom door, he felt relieved to find no one
waiting to get inside. At least he didn't have to feel guilty for trapping
someone in the hallway, doing the pee-pee dance while he uselessly
occupied the porcelain throne. Rolling the notebook into a tube, he
stepped off the bathroom tile onto the wooden floor of the hallway. He

had no problem working through the crowd, though it had grown in the short time he had been hiding in the restroom.

He glanced over his shoulder in time to see Aria give him a little wave. He waved back and wondered again why he hadn't tried harder with her, wishing he hadn't held back when he had the chance. At least, before the accident.

As he got closer to the door, the crowd closed around him, cutting off his view, apparently deciding with subconscious group think that it was time for him to stop looking at Aria. Finally, Jack slipped out the front door into the street, turned right and moved as quickly as he could past the windows, forcing himself not to look into the bar. It was only a few feet to the next building, and then a few feet more to the tattoo parlor with windows he could look into, and even stare at, without feeling regret.

Jack wasn't sure if it was actually colder than when he had entered Liberty's, but the dusky half-dark and the wind in his face made it at least *feel* colder. And more alone. He felt more alone. There was little energy left of the glowing remnants of the day, but Jack was dressed warmly enough to take a lap around the neighborhood. A couple buildings more and he turned right on Fourteenth. He didn't have a hard and fast destination, having so far decided to let the evening carry him where it may in lieu of plotting every detail. The idea was to record the evening in the log, not fill in a day planner, though he suspected he might regret that strategy later. Jack the engineer was not in the habit of *not* planning things.

Fourteenth was narrow, there was only room for parking on one side of the street plus a single lane of one-way traffic. Jack walked against the traffic, catching the last sliver of light fading behind the western hills. He liked walking on Fourteenth. He liked the coziness of it, the four-story buildings pressing in from both sides, forcing human and machine to consider one another and each to make allowances for the other. Jack did not rush westward. He was in no hurry to go nowhere, no hurry to go anywhere. His mood made it easy to enjoy the cool air filling his lungs and sneaking onto his skin through the top of his shirt, drying the moisture that had built up in the heat of Liberty's.

The post-happy-hour/pre-dinner patrons were working their way back to their homes and cars and deciding whether to stay in for the evening or come back later for round two. Jack passed them as they moved around the neighborhood, some in search of randomly parked vehicles, others making bee lines for their homes.

At least for the moment, panhandlers were the only stationary creatures, working passers-by for cash. Jack's habit was to deny he carried cash. This saved him from a less polite response to any begging and carried with it the added benefit of actually being true. At least about half the time. The other half he just lied. He dreaded the day when panhandlers might start carrying mobile credit card processors.

Two blocks later, Jack approached Washington Park and found an empty bench, where he pulled the notebook out of his pocket.

5:45
One thing I won't miss are the panhandlers.
I feel bad for them, but I don't give them money.
I'll buy them a sandwich, maybe a cup of coffee, but no money.
It's the people who don't live down here that give them money.
They don't see them every day.
They don't have to tell three people "no" just walking to their car.
I know they think they're helping them.
Some of these homeless guys are pretty persistent.

They would be great in sales. Just not sure they could pass the drug test.

Okay—that's enough for that rant. I sound like a douchebag.

I'll probably give out a few bucks tonight anyway. Why not?

The park is pretty empty right now. A few kids in the playground.

There's a couple in the gazebo, holding hands.

Sounds like the guy is giving the girl some of the history of Washington Park but I can't hear everything he's saying.

I just see him pointing. Not even sure what he's pointing at.

Could be a tree. Could be a statue.

Hell, he could be pointing at some humping squirrels.

He's definitely not pointing at me.

It doesn't matter, though. She's listening and smiling.

Alright, Posterity, I don't want to sound wimpy here, but you should know there are few things

I find so subtly pleasurable as holding hands with a beautiful girl, even if your hands are sweaty.

It's the connection, I guess. Can't beat it.

Hard not to be a fan of love.

Aria had been uncomfortable ever since Jack departed. It wasn't a physical discomfort, rather a mental one. She hadn't read anything in Jack's notebook that was frightening on its own. In fact, she couldn't really put her finger on the problem. But she was uneasy. It could have been the tone of it, or something he mentioned that flipped a switch in her, but now that Jack was gone, and the notebook along with him, the opportunity to double-check had evaporated. The bar was busy, which she felt was a blessing, as the distraction of the customers helped take her mind off the gnawing feeling in the pit of her stomach.

She tried not to think about it.

But it wasn't working.

No matter how many beers she poured or cocktails she mixed, the gnawing would not subside. There was something wrong, and it had to do with more than the general air of sadness that had been clinging to Jack for the last year. She had grown used to that, had come to accept it as a part of who he was while still hoping, for his sake, that the sadness would eventually loosen its grip. So she went about her job, trying to ignore her intuition, even though the last time she did that the result was disastrous.

Jack looked up from the log, thinking of Lisbeth. Lisbeth, with whom he hadn't spoken since before Valentine's Day. Lisbeth of the beautiful face and smooth, warm body. Things had always been rather unstable between them. Early on, he believed that this instability added to the excitement of their relationship. Jack had never been with anyone who could be as giving as Lisbeth, or as cold, and he struggled to be properly accepting of the former and to make sense of the latter. Over time, of course, the struggle became tedious for them both. In the end, the unstable foundation of the relationship simply couldn't bear the added weight of the accident, the weight of his guilt and anger. The weight of a little boy's body.

5:51

Well, Posterity.

Let me tell you something about Lisbeth.

She is the ex-girlfriend. Well, the most recent ex-girlfriend.

There've been other ex-girlfriends, of course. I mean, I haven't really lived the life of a monk.

But Lisbeth was the most intense. Lisbeth was a force to be reckoned with.

She could love me so fiercely I found it frightening and I would pull back.

The result of me pulling back was that I got to see her other side, the side that was far less fun.

The side that was frightening for other, ugly, reasons.

I don't blame her really. I'm sure I appeared to be as hot and cold to her as she was to me.

I've read that behind every crazy woman is a frustrating man.

I probably deserved to get kicked to the curb.

Jack stopped to read his words and look for mistakes. To his surprise, he didn't find any, or at least didn't recognize any, but was again impressed by his progress on the pages. He had written more than ten by then and smiled as he silently joked about the size of his writing.

Writing smaller certainly would have resulted in fewer completed pages, but it hardly mattered. Jack had no lofty delusions about the eventual audience for his log.

From its inception, the "Drunk Log" was intended as a utilitarian exercise, meant for himself first, and then perhaps other close family members. It was not destined for *The New York Times* Best Seller List.

Jack laughed aloud at that notion.

While he wrote, what was left of the natural glow of the sun failed completely, plunging the park into darkness and awakening the pole lamps. While Jack felt somewhat displeased by the loss of the day, he enjoyed the effect the lights had on the park. The onset of the night hadn't reduced the number of people there; it just made them, and everything around them, look and feel different. Suddenly, no one in the park existed, at least not until they emerged from the darkness and passed through one of the halos created by the electric bulbs. But their existence was temporary. As soon as they escaped the halo, they were sucked back into the darkness, where the existence of their corporeal selves could again be called into question.

Jack smiled at his little game, realizing he might not be playing it but for the three drinks consumed before leaving Liberty's. His thoughts were generally more creative when under the influence, or so he believed, although he wasn't sure if this was due to some direct effect of the alcohol or because the booze simply gave him license to allow his creativity to come to the fore. In the end, the effect was the same, and the cause irrelevant.

His musings on the interplay of light in the park complete, Jack picked up the pen to declare an entirely new take on the weather.

5:55
It's getting colder now that the sun has disappeared.
I can feel the cold coming up through the bench into my ass.
It's not necessarily unpleasant, at least not yet.
This is a nice place to write, Posterity. On a bench in the halo
of a park lamp.
You should try it some time, at least after its warmer.
Nobody is looking over my shoulder.
I suppose some curious pedestrian could waddle over and take
a peek before I noticed them.
It is dark, after all. I guess I would have to say something to
them,
since Aria's not here to get them to fuck off. Speaking of Aria . .
.

Fuck!
Stop it.

Sorry, Posterity. I'll try to stay focused.
Okay, back to the park. And the cold in my ass. And the people
wandering in and out of the light.
From where I'm sitting, I'm not more than a two-minute walk
from at least six bars.
I know that that statement really doesn't have anything to do
with the park,
other than to highlight its central location.
I mean, I could quite literally throw a rock and hit a couple of
them.
Again, not about the park, but it's kind of interesting, isn't it?
Plus, all those choices make my job that much harder.
I suppose I could try to get to all of them, but that just seems
crazy.
Nope. One at a time. That's my rule tonight.
Well, at least ONE of my rules. I'm sure I made a few I don't
even remember.

Jack stopped writing and looked around. From his vantage point he could see Vestry, a small bar on the ground floor of an old church that had been converted to an event space but was also open to the public. Jack didn't know why he hadn't thought of it already. After all, it was a spot he could have hit with a rock. Almost. If he had a better throwing arm.

Without any more thought, Jack closed the notebook, stood up and left the park. Before entering the bar, he took a moment to glance in the window and was pleased to see the interior sparsely populated, which convinced him he had made a good choice.

Though Vestry was not large, there were a few tables scattered about for those wishing to skip the bar or mill about with drinks in their hands.

Jack took advantage of the bar's current lack of patronage and selected a table in the corner, equidistant between the front door and the bar, a spot he believed would provide him the highest level of privacy currently available. Though the public side of the bar was not busy, there was a wedding reception taking place on the floor above, and guests had spilled over on the other side of the bar. Jack noted the rope separating two areas of the bar, the public and private. Ostensibly, the rope provided a barrier of sufficient physical and psychological heft to keep the two sides from blending. The last thing the Father of the Bride needed was to have the bar tab run up by opportunistic reception crashers.

Initially assuming he would need to go to the bar to order his drink, Jack was surprised to find the bartender standing next to him, as if he had just appeared in a puff of smoke. But Jack was happy to be waited on. With table service, he could lounge in a chair, having his drinks brought to him. It wasn't that Jack minded ordering drinks from the bar, because normally he was fine with that, but on that evening he was especially appreciative of being waited on.

"What can I get for you?"

The bartender was smiling. His near-magical arrival caught Jack off-guard. He wasn't quite sure what he wanted, and though the bartender didn't appear to be in any hurry, Jack still felt pressured. Suddenly, and with no intervention on the part of his conscious brain, he listened as his voice asked for a glass of red wine. For Jack, this resembled an out-of-body experience, as he hadn't put any thought into that choice. It just popped out of his mouth like some alien force had made him say it.

Red wine? Do I even like red wine?

The hyper-efficient bartender managed to scoot back behind the bar before Jack had a chance to change his mind.

Okay, that's fine, I guess. I can blame Fate for my drink order.

For Jack, Fate's intervention meant the glass of wine must have a higher purpose, one for which he was as yet unaware, but one which undoubtedly existed. Jack found the thought comforting and pulled out the notebook to write about it as the waiter reappeared with the wine.

Aria knew she was going to reach a breaking point. She understood her efforts to *not* act on the feeling of dread growing inside of her had so far been unsuccessful. But what was she to do? She was stuck behind the bar until closing. By then, she figured, all manner of unpleasant outcomes were possible, and by now, just a half hour or so after Jack's departure, she was imagining just about all of them. They were all bad.

She knew what she had to do. She knew there was only one way to fight what she was feeling. She was going to have to look for Jack. She was going to have to find him and make sure he was alright, and, if he wasn't, then it was even more important she be with him. She didn't know exactly why; she just knew she had to.

Aria grabbed her cell phone from her purse and called Aaron, who was not scheduled to work that night. They had become friends over the last year, and she knew enough about him to suspect his plans for the evening likely involved hiding in his apartment, reading, until he fell asleep. He would be available.

He answered his phone on the first ring.

In her mind, Aria was already on her way, one step closer to some slice of salvation, whether hers or Jack's or both.

Chapter Five

Bar Fight

The screaming stopped. When it did, Jack was no longer sure he existed in the silence that flooded in as the last scream faded. All he could feel was the pressure of Troy's body against his. Jack heard sound and movement coming from outside the cloistered cabin of the Camry, but it echoed as if he were stuck inside a tunnel. Somewhere, at the end of the tunnel, there was hope, maybe, and even light. Somewhere, beyond the wave of despair crashing upon him, there was help. Maybe. The boy's body was sinking into his own. Still the voices.

> *6:06*
> *I was going to say something about the fate thing,*
> *but I'm not sure I want to go down that rabbit hole.*
> *I mean, if fate is a real thing, then how am I responsible for*
> *anything?*
> *In a way, it's a nice thought, this idea that I'm really not re-*
> *sponsible for the good or the bad, that it's all in the hands of*
> *something else.*
> *But if it's true, if it's all pre-ordained, then why bother?*
> *Smarter people than me have thought this through already.*
> *Okay, Posterity, you're right.*
> *I went down the rabbit hole, but only a little. I'm back now.*
> *Getting back to the other thing: I suppose if I'm going to riff*
> *on the nature of love when it comes to Lisbeth, I might as*
> *well talk about Troy, too.*

I never wondered if I loved him. I've never wondered if he loved me.
It was all very straightforward.
All he ever wanted to do was hang out with his uncle.
All he ever wanted to do was whatever I was doing.
It was easy to make him happy. All I had to do was let him hang around. Around me, I mean.
And I could be doing anything.
Cleaning the apartment, cooking dinner, or working on the computer.
He didn't care as long as it was just the two of us.
Now that's unconditional love for you.
He didn't even complain.
Well, not as much as you'd think a little boy would complain if he was forced to sit and watch his uncle work on a computer.
Might as well make him eat liver, too.
But he usually found ways to amuse himself.
He'd read (sort of,) or work on a puzzle, or watch some TV.
Whatever it was, he was willing to do it until I was done with whatever I was doing.

Jack set the pen down and took a sip of wine. He hadn't had a glass of wine in months. In the pantheon of available alcohol, wine was rarely his first choice. For Jack, wine was almost always an afterthought, an idea that occurred to him after a few beers or a cocktail, or if someone else ordered it for him.

Oh, look at that. May as well drink it.

This night wasn't any different than the others, other than on this particular evening he was drinking alone in an empty corner of a nearly empty bar. Jack did not feel lonely, however. To the contrary, he was complimenting himself on this choice of venue and seating.

In the corner of that small bar, he was finding inspiration, though he was not consciously aware he was searching for anything more than the next drink and another page filled in his notebook.

He did recognize a shift in his vision, a shift in his soul. In his corner, for some reason, the world was feeling bigger than it had before he sat down. He liked the feeling. It was not new. It had just been a while since he had felt it.

"How's the wine?"

Jack was startled by the bartender. Had he come up through a trap door in the floor?

"It's good, thanks."

Jack looked up at the bartender, who was smiling and standing motionless next to the small table. The bartender's calm demeanor indicated he was in no hurry to return to his designated area, behind the bar. Indeed, he seemed to crave conversation, which was the exact opposite of what Jack was seeking, sitting alone, on purpose.

The possibility occurred to Jack that he just had nothing better to do. The bar was slow, after all, and maybe he should try to be nice.

"Um, I'll let you know if I need anything?"

It didn't sound as nice as Jack had hoped.

"Oh, great. Okay."

The bartender, sensing the end of an awkward conversation, immediately retreated back to the bar and its other two patrons, who were perhaps more welcoming of his overtures.

For his part, and wishing the bartender no ill will, Jack could not help being annoyed. His meditation had been disturbed. For him, the fourth drink was nearly always the one that slowed the churning of the world, at least just a bit, and gave long-buried thoughts a chance to be heard. It was often fleeting, that moment when he was able to let things go, and sometimes nearly imperceptible, and so he was anxious to capture it, especially on this night.

In an attempt to throw himself back into the moment, he took a deep breath and refocused his attention on the glass, thinking he may have misjudged his odds of being interrupted in a small, empty bar. Working to tamp down his ire, Jack reminded himself that the bartender was just trying to be attentive, a thought which miraculously allowed his neck muscles to loosen.

The glass of red wine hadn't moved during the entire ordeal with the bartender, taking no notice of the interaction, none at all, at least not as far as Jack could tell. Certainly, not only had the glass remained motion-less during their stilted conversation, the level of its contents had neither grown nor receded. The wine, and the glass holding it, remained quietly unaltered.

Jack found odd comfort in the inevitability of the fact that inanimate objects would not and could not modify themselves without his interven-tion and pondered this as he took another sip. Once the glass was safely returned to its perch on the small table in front of him, he rediscovered the moment he feared the bartender had stolen. Staring at the wine, Jack allowed himself to fall into it. Every breath took him deeper into the glass. Every breath. Deeper.

Aria was clock watching and, despite the clock's indication to the contrary, she was sure it had been an hour since Aaron promised to relieve her in thirty minutes. At least an hour. Maybe more. Where the hell was he? And why was the damn clock moving so slowly? Aria did her best to fend off the vague sense of panic fogging around her and continued working diligently, but she needed the hour to be over in less than sixty minutes. She needed a math miracle and wordlessly commanded the clock to move faster.

It had occurred to her, some ten minutes earlier, that she might be crazy. After all, whatever relationship she and Jack had built over the last couple years almost exclusively revolved around him giving her money in exchange for alcohol. No doubt they had learned a good deal about each other during the time they had spent across the bar from one another, but beyond the kiss, there wasn't much more to be gleaned from a casual relationship between a bartender and a regular.

But, she thought, there *was* something. There was definitely something more. She knew about Jack's parents and his brother, and she had met the boy one afternoon when Jack brought him into the bar. And he knew things about her, too. He knew she graduated college right after she started working at Liberty's. He knew it took her five years to get a four-year degree because she didn't, she simply couldn't, decide on a major until her fourth year. And they both knew each of them was attracted to the other. It was a good kiss, after all.

Where the hell was Aaron?

As Jack sank deeper into the wine, his mind wandered to places rarely travelled in the last few months. It wasn't a violent or unwelcome wandering. In fact, Jack's brain was taking him on a rather pleasant tour of good memories, or at least mostly good memories. He was fine with a few not-so-good memories, ones his brain allowed to sneak in, at least in the moment. He wasn't in a mood to question. He was alone in the corner, swimming around in a glass of wine, with a Do Not Disturb sign written all over him.

6:14

I can't believe how good I feel right now. Haven't felt this good in months.

I forgot how good the fourth drink could be, at least most of the time.

I mean, if you're in a shitty mood and then have another drink, there's no guarantee another drink won't make you less shitty, and in actuality will probably just make you shittier.

But I must have picked the right moment.

Did I mention how amazing I feel?

Honestly, I think I'll be good for as long as the glass of wine holds out,

at least as long as the bar doesn't fill up.

If that happens, I'm in the right position to have a lot of asses in my face.

Don't get me wrong, having asses in my face isn't necessarily a bad thing.

Hell, under the right circumstances it can be a damn good thing.

But I don't think that that's what will be happening tonight, alas.

(Did you notice the last word of the last sentence? Looks like I start writing like Shakespeare after the third drink.)

Jack took a moment to review his most recent entry. Not his best, he decided, but passable. Taking a moment to riffle the pages, he guessed he had seventy or eighty to go in order to finish and wasn't quite sure if he had it in him. As he attempted to calculate the number of words needed to finish the journal, the bar was invaded with what appeared to be seven or eight college students. The clearly inebriated group breezed past Jack without acknowledging his presence, a fact he appreciated, sitting as he was on his little island in the corner of the room. It wasn't until a loud argument broke out between two of the young literati that Jack began to fear for his hard-earned solitude.

"I told you, fuckhead, she's a slut."

It was obvious to Jack that this particular student was not majoring in English or Rhetoric, and certainly not Bar Diplomacy.

"And I told *you* not to call my girlfriend a slut!"

"I'm not *calling* her a slut. I'm *telling* you she's a slut. She's fucked half the guys at the fraternity! Look man, I'm just trying to look out for you."

With some measure of alarm, Jack observed the boyfriend of the alleged skank make an aggressive move toward his somewhat smaller companion. It appeared the presumed slut's boyfriend did not seem at all convinced his companion was just trying to "look out for him." Their voices were only getting louder and body language more threatening. Jack, of course, just wanted them to leave, though he had no plan for implementing this desire and, somewhat alarmingly, the altercation had moved away from the bar, now unfolding just three feet from him and his glass of wine. Quickly comprehending he was planted well within the danger zone, Jack turned back to the journal and glass of wine with an eye to protecting both from what he suspected was about to come flying their way. But it was too late. Before he could get his fingers around the glass, the body of the tramp-accuser flew over Jack's left shoulder, landing directly onto the table which had, just seconds before, held half a glass of wine and his log.

Jack was examining the wreckage when the randy debutante's boyfriend proceeded to fling himself down upon his classmate, eliminating any possibility the table could ever be fixed in the future.

As the two struggled over the honor of the accused harlot, Jack could do nothing but stand to the side and wait for them to wear each other down, thereby giving him the opportunity to recover the notebook without risking undue injury to himself. The wine glass had disappeared and was no doubt in shards beneath the bodies of the struggling young men, perhaps trying to burrow some piece of itself into one or both of their backs in a mindless quest for revenge.

Regardless, Jack's wait-and-see gambit was foiled by the other students, who appeared to have taken sides in the dust-up. With the remaining scholars evenly split on the social status of the girl in question, the original mano-y-mano conflict grew into a conflagration, bodies flying about the bar in the style of an old Western. In spite of the escalating fracas, Jack managed to maintain his focus on the search for the notebook, at least until one of the flying bodies was unintentionally blocked by his own.

The other man wasn't so much flying as he was stumbling backward and Jack, who for all intents and purposes was minding his own business as much as anyone could under the circumstances, was taken completely by surprise. Before he knew what happened, he found himself on the bottom of a growing heap of drunken man-flesh but, as luck would have it, this was not Jack's first experience with a multiple-participant bar fight, and would not be his last. He did not panic, and instead worked methodically to get to his hands and knees, with an eye toward rising to a full standing position.

Jack was not, however, fully cognizant of the two groups' intense aspirations to overcome one another. Usually, in a fight of this kind, the players' passions burn out fairly quickly, leaving them in a sort of quiet satisfaction as the initial burst of adrenaline recedes along with the desire to smash the face of whoever happens to be standing closest.

In this fight, however, the opposite seemed to be occurring, and as the level of violence increased so did the anger and determination of those involved. The result of this sustained passion, from Jack's perspective, was the level of difficulty it imposed on his efforts to get vertical, and he found himself getting knocked to the ground each time he tried to pull himself up from a squat. He was not pleased, but he had little choice other than to keep trying. Almost unbelievably, Jack was sustaining no personal injury. He just kept getting knocked down before he had a chance to look for the notebook.

The bartender, being the only representative of the establishment available to stem the tide of falling bodies, was rendered powerless in the effort by the sheer number of actors involved, and so dialed the police as soon as his survival instincts overcame his initial sense of disbelief at the scene unfolding before him.

Eventually, and before the police even had a chance to roust the place, the student-warriors did indeed run out of steam, giving Jack the opportunity to look for the notebook.

Considering what he had just been through, Jack conducted his search with surprising restraint, only having to kick one lay-about in the ass and drag another by the legs two or three yards before finding the journal under the head of a student whose nose had clearly been broken. The bloody spurt that had found its way from the broken nose to the cover of the Drunk Log did not disturb Jack at all, in fact it pleased him. Much like the water stains earlier in the evening, the drying blood from the mashed face of the spent student only added to the character of the journal.

My drunk and bloody log, Jacked mused. Examining it with a smile, he made a mental note to explain the blood stain in a log entry, for Posterity.

60

Considering the scene around him, once the log was recovered Jack no longer felt any obligation to remain in The Vestry. Stepping over prone figures, he stood at the bar, card in hand, ready to pay his tab. The bartender, phone to his ear, was still receiving instructions from the 911 operator.

"How much do I owe you?"

Jack's tone was matter-of-fact. He was far less flustered than the bartender, likely because he wasn't worried about whether he'd still have a job the next day.

"Um . . . it's on the house. Cool?"

The bartender had put his hand over the receiver as if to shield the 911 operator from the incidental financial conversation he was having with one of the nonviolent patrons.

"You're sure?"

Jack still had his credit card in hand, poised to insert it into the chip reader as soon as he had permission to do so.

"Yup . . . absolutely sure."

"Well, okay then. Awesome. Thanks."

Jack turned on his heel and exited the bar just as the police were arriving. It did not occur to him that they might want to question him about what had just transpired. Luckily, the police seemed to discount his level of culpability in the disturbance, allowing him to walk right past them on his way out. He did not *feel* guilty, at least not about the bar fight, and his lack of guilt surely shone brightly as he walked back out into the neighborhood. There was still the matter of the loss of a half-glass of wine, but there was nothing Jack could do about it until he got to another bar.

Aaron finally showed up to relieve Aria, and by the time he arrived she was nearly out of her shoes.

"Jesus Christ, Aaron. Don't think I don't appreciate you doing this for me, but what the hell took you so long?"

She was waving one of those long bar spoons in his face, the kind you use to mix drinks in tall glasses. Aaron feared she might smack him in the face.

"Jeez! Sorry, Aria. I got here as fast as I could. I had to shower and . . ."

"Shower? Really, Aaron? How did I manage to pick your shower day to ask you for a favor?"

The spoon was still threatening.

"Now, c'mon Aria. Is that really called for?"

It dawned on Aria that she was wasting time and, besides, everybody knew Aaron took plenty of showers. She was just being mean.

"Okay, you're right. Sorry."

To Aaron's relief, Aria handed him the spoon.

"I'm out. I owe you."

"Yeah, you do."

Aaron was smiling, but he was talking to her back. She was out the door before he finished.

Aria kept a light jacket hidden under the bar and grabbed it as she exited, entering the darkness without a real plan to find Jack.

Okay, the neighborhood is not that big. I just need to be methodical.

She suspected Jack would stay in Over the Rhine, so she broke the street grid down, picturing it in her mind. Most of the bars were concentrated on two or three streets in the district. She decided she would start with those. To Aria, the task was not as daunting as it might have been for others. Because of the hours and the nature of their jobs, bar and restaurant workers were a tightly knit family of sorts. She knew she could walk into almost any bar in the neighborhood and find someone willing to help her. She headed south on Main, less anxious, now that she was in action.

Chapter Six

Vice and Other Drugs

As the sound and fury faded, Jack's hearing began to recover. Now he could distinguish voices leaking in through the shattered glass. He heard a noise he understood to be a siren. It was loud. It was loud enough that he was able to focus only on the sound of it and believe that help was coming. In that moment there was also hope, but the hope wouldn't last long. The boy's body was too heavy.

> *6:34*
> *I'm sitting in the park again, just across the street from the Vestry.*
> *I don't know why I keep ending up here.*
> *Probably because it's shorter to walk through the park than around it,*
> *or maybe because there are benches to sit on. Doesn't matter, really.*
> *What really matters is where I decide to go next, and I don't know where that will be.*
> *I could leave the neighborhood and just go downtown now, but I have so many pages left to fill.*
> *I'm not even halfway done.*

Jack slipped through the throng of Cincinnati police as if he were a ghost. All the cops were ostensibly engaged in one cop-like activity or another, either questioning witnesses or those involved in the fight itself, but Jack may as well have been invisible. He liked it that way and was mostly happy to be across the street and away from all the rumpus around the bar.

Having successfully escaped the obnoxious scrum, Jack smiled at the aftermath of the collegiate intra-fraternity bar fight. He wasn't responsible for the scene, but he had to admit that he enjoyed its composition, its chaos.

For a moment he thought it might be fun to walk back across the street and invite an interview. After all, he really had been in the thick of things, and had something of an "insider's" view of the melee that had unfolded around him, but he decided against reinserting himself into that story. No good would come of it, he believed, and he had more important things to do anyway. Still, he walked away feeling a tad torn. It had looked like fun over there, especially if one stood little chance of ending up in handcuffs.

The Vestry was only a block from the edge of the neighborhood, but Jack wasn't yet ready to go, to "breach its boundaries." That would come later, he knew, when he was drunker, and the night darker. He turned his back to the church, deciding his next drink would be dispensed at Sundry and Vice, at least as long as it wasn't too busy, at least busy to the point where he would be distracted from his own thoughts, his own purpose.

Surrounded by the flashes of red and blue still radiating from the police cruisers behind him, Jack wound his way back through the park. Sundry and Vice was off the edge of the other side, and he was close enough that he believed he could see its outline just beyond the shadows through which he was walking.

Had Jack wandered into Sundry & Vice later in the evening, he likely would have been disappointed by the large crowd. But that swell wouldn't form for another hour or more, so for now there were still bar seats and a booth available for anyone who wanted them. As quickly as he could, or at least as quickly as he could manage without looking like a child trying to grab the last cookie, Jack slid into the booth and laid the notebook in front of him.

Despite the dim light, Jack could see that the notebook had indeed suffered some contusions during its time on the floor, being crushed by boozy assailants. The cover now registered some creases that had not existed before the Vestry, and in addition to the blood spatter on the front there was a prominent wet stain on the back. The light was insufficient for a full analysis of the stain, but he suspected it came from his own wine glass, though considering the extenuating circumstances, he didn't hold himself responsible. Instead, Jack laid the blame squarely on the shoulders of the soused schoolboys. The notebook would survive, certainly, and neither blood nor wine had as yet penetrated the cover or imperiled any of the words inside.

His inspection complete, Jack gave the bar a once-over. The age of the crowd varied between those just beginning to drink legally and those solidly beyond an age when identification might be necessary. The music was playing but was not so intrusive as to preclude anyone from having a non-yelling conversation. He knew that would change later, as the bar filled. He also knew he would be moving on long before that happened. For now, he just needed a drink.

Sundry & Vice produced certain cocktails en masse and served them from taps behind the bar. Fancying himself a purist, Jack did not easily warm to the idea of mass-produced cocktails poured from a tap but, after trying an Old Fashioned, he was happy to revise his expectations. Since it was still early enough in his drinking regimen to care about what he slid over his taste buds, Jack knew this was as good a choice as any. He got his drink, sat down in his recently acquired booth, and opened up the log.

6:43

Sorry about the damage, Posterity. Couldn't be helped.

I was literally minding my own business in the Vestry when it was invaded

by a bunch of dumbasses who would sooner belong in a cage than in a classroom.

Go figure.

Back to drinking . . . and using up space with dots and extra spaces that don't really belong.

You know, I'd love to talk about drinking more, but I am running out of things to say.

I mean, this (Old Fashioned) is a good drink and all, but maybe you're tired of hearing about it.

Fuck, maybe I'm tired of hearing about it.

But, if this is going to be a Drunk Log, I guess I'd better keep writing about drinking.

On that note . . . I believe I'm actually a little less buzzy than I was when I went into the Vestry.

I think it's because all the commotion gave me a shot of adrenaline

that's working against the alcohol I've so carefully consumed all evening.

This isn't an issue except for when it comes to time.

I may now have to drink more than I thought and, quite honestly,

I don't want to have to be out late enough to close any bars.

At some point this all has to come to an end.

Eventually I'll run out of paper, I hope.

Maybe that will be the end of it.

Jack put the pen down, took a sip of the drink and gathered his thoughts, the most prominent of which was that he had to urinate, followed by the fact that he didn't want to urinate. He didn't want to pee for fear of additional sins being committed against the cover of the notebook. Jack felt the notebook had suffered enough, at least for now, and so he would not release it from his possession again. He had come to believe he had no way to guarantee its safety, not once he carried it into an environment full of urinals, toilets, and wet counters. He pondered the situation, coming to the conclusion that a solution for his dilemma would present itself if he didn't try too hard to find one.

Aria had begun to question what she was doing and why she was doing it. It all started with a feeling, a feeling that had swept over her while she and Jack were in the bar together, and that feeling had only intensified since his departure. Reading the log had made her uneasy, and not just because she was violating his privacy. Had she put any thought into it all, had she spent just a little more time trying to understand what she was feeling, she likely wouldn't have left the bar. She knew this, but here she was, searching for him in the darkness without any clue as to where he might be. By her estimation, there were at least thirty bars in Over-the-Rhine alone, and many more if she was forced to take into account all the bars still within walking distance, despite being outside the boundaries of the neighborhood where, she guessed, Jack would probably remain.

She was in the dark, searching for . . . what?

It occurred to her, just before she stepped into Mr. Pitiful's, that she might be in love with Jack, although she didn't know *why* she might be in love with him. Aria had been in love before, most certainly, and knew what it felt like, even when she didn't always want to feel it. She had felt love's desperation, its cruelty. Her last relationship, an experiment with a man twenty years her senior, was the direct result of the failed love that had come before.

The older man was nice enough, and emotionally stable, but often seemed to be embarrassed by their age difference. This embarrassment would manifest itself in a number of ways, most noticeably when he would introduce her as his "friend." By the same token, Aria could never bring herself to introduce him to her parents, as they were only six years or so older than him.

But the thing that really bugged her was a thing she considered shallow, and something she was never quite able to admit to herself, even though it started getting under her skin less than two months into the relationship. It was his paunch. Some part of Aria was bugged by the fact that he was getting fat before she was ready to do the same.

Now, she had no intention of getting fat for at least another twenty-five years or so. She felt that, if one was going to get fat, they should at least wait until their fifties, and should definitely have had children. That was kind of a given for her. But, she figured, by that time he would be seventy and, due to an ever-burgeoning waistline, likely trapped in an iron chair, or something along those lines. So, despite the fact that he was always polite, had a good job, and was more than adequate in bed, she knew she couldn't stay with him, so she didn't. Besides, the simple truth was that Aria and her elderly beau were not in love, and this made the breakup surprisingly easy for both of them.

Jack, on the other hand, was only four or five years older than Aria, and there was clearly a mutual attraction. But she believed there was more to it than that, or else there was no way she would have found herself standing at the bar at Mr. Pitiful's, conducting an interrogation on an unsuspecting and busy bartender about the possible whereabouts of a man he didn't know.

Aria received, with some disdain, an "I know nothing" shoulder shrug from the bartender, whom she now felt was most likely an idiot. After all, how could he not sense the urgency of the situation? Failing at her first sleuthing attempt did not deter her at all, however, and it took only a few seconds to consider her options. She knew what she would do. She would keep looking. She would follow her instincts.

She would take a chance.

Halfway into the Old Fashioned, Jack still had not gone to the bathroom, in spite of the internal pressure building in his bladder and his mind. Finally, though, he was forced to yield. He folded the log in half and jammed it into his back pocket, figuring the potential damage produced by the folding and jamming was less dire than potentially introducing bodily fluids to its pages. It was, in Jack's mind, even less dire than someone reading it before it was ready to be read.

Jack mostly understood that, should he leave the log on the table, there was little chance that a random passerby would pick it up and start reading it. Few people were so boorish. Still, he wasn't ready to take the chance. So, with the notebook secure against his hind quarters, Jack ventured to the restroom, stepped to the urinal and examined the floor for puddles of God-knows-what, anything quietly lying-in-wait for notebooks falling out of pants pockets.

Satisfied the floor was sufficiently liquid-free, Jack was able to relax and do his business. The only distraction was a yellowed prescription, written in the scrawl of a long-dead pharmacist, trapped in a shadowbox above the urinal. In keeping with the apothecary theme, the owner decorated the entire bar with paraphernalia one might find in a hundred-plus-year-old drug store. Jack enjoyed trying to make out the prescription, which happened to be for laudanum. Despite having made a number of trips to this particular toilet, he had yet to decipher the scrawl, and would fail to do so again on this night. His failure did not dampen his enthusiasm for the task, however, and he stared at the old script until jarred from his reverie by another patron attempting to enter the single-person restroom through the locked door. Having finished what he had gone there to do, Jack zipped his pants and exited.

"All yours."

Jack almost smiled as he spoke to the patient young lady waiting for him to slide past her.

"Thanks."

She smiled up at him before disappearing behind the bathroom door.

After washing his hands at the communal sink, Jack obsessive-compulsively reached for the notebook, making sure it was still jammed into his back pocket. It was still there, and with that knowledge he breathed a sigh of relief and slid back into the booth where the Old Fashioned waited patiently for its owner.

The bar was still only half-full, so Jack felt sufficiently confident to again put pen to paper, but paused before doing so.

What am I writing about?

Something about my past?

Perhaps something about a screwed up parental relationship?

He initially discarded the latter out of hand. Everyone had a screwed-up-parental-relationship story. If not that, however, what then? Feelings of being alone? Universal themes one and all. What could he write that was worth reading? What could he write that was worth Posterity's time?

"Fuck it."

Jack took a swig and picked up his pen.

6:49

So, here's something.

After the accident, my mom wouldn't talk to me for months.

She blamed me for killing her grandson.

She's right to blame me, of course—I did kill him.

So maybe it's right that she never talks to me again.

At the funeral, she wouldn't even look at me.

I think Dad has tried to smooth things over,

but so far I haven't received any invitations to Thanksgiving,

so it doesn't look like he's making much headway.

Not sure I'd want to go anyway.

It would just make everyone uncomfortable, including me.

It's okay, Posterity. I deserve it.

If this were the old days, I mean the hundreds-of-years-ago old days,

they would have stuck me in the stocks and let people throw rotten fruit and vegetables at me.

I wonder if Mom would feel better if I let her throw rotten stuff at me.

I did kill her grandson, after all.

Jack paused, took another drink, and let the alcohol wash over him. The gift of adrenaline he received from the bar fight had waned, giving the alcohol a chance to settle back in. He stared at the page and sipped the drink, trying to make sure he was gauging its effect on him but not having much luck. His own hormone production was skewing the expected results of his steady consumption, and though he was not even close to besotted, at least by his standards, he was, indeed, more shit-faced than he realized.

6:52

Wow, Posterity.

I just read what I just wrote and it's pretty depressing.

Let's talk about something more fun, like drinking. Or maybe not.

Honestly, I'm not sure what to put down here at the moment.

Seems like all the subjects I've got to talk about are mostly depressing.

But you know what, fuck it.

It's my log—I'll write about whatever I want, and Posterity can suck it.

I was thinking the other day about how I took something away from my brother and sister-in-law.

Okay, I mean, I took something other than their son.

It isn't only that they lost their child, but also all the stuff that was going to go with it,

with parenthood, I mean. It's not just the kid, it's all the stuff that goes with the kid.

All the time together, all the joy and anger and frustration that I know has to come along with having one. I mean, I don't know first-hand, but there's plenty of parents at work talking about all the shit that goes on with their kids, good and bad. And that's what I took away.

I even took away their guilt, you know what I mean?

I took away the guilt that I think all parents feel at some point.

I don't know. Parents always seem to feel guilty about something.

Guilty that they didn't let their kid go to a sleepover.

Guilty they didn't save enough for college.

Guilty that they burned the macaroni and cheese.

Seems like parents who give a shit are always feeling guilty
about something.
And that's what I took. I took all of the good and bad stuff
from them,
and I replaced it with anger at me. And it's just too much.

Jack put the pen down and drank half of what remained of the Old Fashioned. He was starting to feel the way he thought he should have felt by then, after five potent drinks. This was normal, he told himself, for five drinks. This is finally how he should be feeling, except that under normal circumstances he would be enjoying the buzz more fully, enjoying the lightness-of-being that the alcohol carried with it into his bloodstream and psyche. He was trying to enjoy it. He felt he should, on this night of all nights. But instead, he was staring down at his words, reliving the most nightmarish moment of his entire existence, and could not stop himself from giving in all over again to the sadness.

Aria made her way to Central Parkway, to the edge of the neighborhood, and stopped. A light snow began to fall. It was early in the season for snow. It wasn't sticking yet. The ground probably wasn't cold enough. Still, it was the first of the season and she loved snow, so she took a moment to stand in it and let it settle on her knit cap and light wool jacket before pulling herself back to the task at hand.

This corner contained no bars. It was, instead occupied by a parking lot, a government building, and a derelict hulk that used to be a furniture store. The barren monstrosity, now empty for years, had at some point become a home for drug users and the homeless before it was completely secured from intruders. Now it just sat there, slouching over Aria's presently motionless form, serving no real purpose other than to take up space.

Aria tried to ignore the surroundings and remain focused on her mission. She gave in to the snow for a few more moments before considering her options, which were myriad. She listed them in her head: 1. Turn around and go home. 2. Turn around and go back to work. 3. Take a break from the search and grab a slice at one of the pizza joints she had passed on her way to this empty corner. She liked number three the best. Both pizza joints were equipped with full-service bars so she could kill two birds with one stone, satisfy her hunger *and* fulfill her desire to question bartenders about Jack's possible whereabouts. She liked the efficiency of her choice and the fact that it meant she wasn't giving up. Not yet.

I've never been a giver-upper, she told herself, *and I'm not going to start now.*

Standing in line at the counter, Aria wondered what her parents would say about what she was doing. She had cultivated a habit of telling her parents nearly everything. *Nearly* everything. She never told them about the old guy. That would have been a disaster. Though loving, they weren't terribly accepting of "different" as a rule and learning of their daughter's affair with a man almost twice her age would likely have resulted in much wailing and gnashing of teeth, not to mention incessant questioning and borderline judgment. She had always considered them overprotective, especially since they lost her sister, Steffie. Things got worse after that.

It had taken them a year, after all, just to quit bugging her about moving into her place in Over the Rhine, a former slum still only half gentrified after 15 years of effort by the city. What she and her friends saw as a beautiful, diverse neighborhood in transition for the better was viewed by her parents as a place that should be permanently wrapped in police tape. So, she didn't tell them everything. And she certainly wasn't ever going to tell them about the little adventure in which she was presently engaged.

What if they meet Jack some day?

Aria figured that with all her family had been through losing Steffie, she couldn't have this "situation" with Jack hanging over their heads, too.

Jeez. What do I do now?

She ordered her slice and went to the bar to get a beer and ask some questions.

Chapter Seven

Black and White Russians

The voices were gone. Or at least he couldn't hear them anymore. The voices were replaced by a sustained whirring and the groan of steel being forcibly detached from itself. It occurred to him he may have lost consciousness for a few seconds or more because he could not pinpoint the exact moment when the voices were lost, overwhelmed by the sound of tearing metal, but all he could do was stare forward at the shattered windshield.

6:58
I see snowflakes through the window. Not sure when that happened.
It's early in the year for that. I like it though.
I like that it's snowing tonight, of all nights.
Don't worry, Posterity, I'm not attaching any special meaning to it.
I don't think the universe is reaching out to me through a bunch of snowflakes.
Now, if I go outside and those flakes have magically formed a coherent message on the sidewalk, in English, then maybe I'll rethink my position on the universe, or God,
trying to speak to me through an unusual weather pattern.
And it would have to be straightforward and to the point.
I don't want to have to solve any riddles.

I've got to get out into it, however. The snow, I mean.

My glass is empty, so it's time to move on.

One drink per bar. That's sort of my rule, in case I failed to mention it earlier.

I know, Posterity. I broke my own rule right off the bat.

I'm pretty sure Aria made me three drinks, but I'll have to go back through my notes and review. What drink number am I drinking? Well, actually I mean . . . what number did I just drink? Five?

I mean I'm not drinking it anymore because I finished it and it's time to move on.

Jeez. I'm really feeling it right now.

Maybe I need to slow down for a little bit. I really need to check my notes.

I don't want to lose count and fuck this all up.

For some reason, I think the count is important, but maybe it's only important to me.

But please don't ask why, Posterity. I don't have the answer right now.

When I do, you'll be the first to know.

Jack stopped writing, folded the log and put it in his back pocket. In the time it took him to perform that action, he also managed to forget about the plan to audit his intake so that he could figure out where he was in the drink order.

In the time it took to slip into his coat and step into the snow, the need for doing that had completely escaped him. By then, however, it was too late for him to take on such a task. It was too dark to see his words, and besides, the pages of the notebook were too susceptible to the moisture of the falling flakes.

None of this yet occurred to Jack, who was enjoying the cool of the outside and the contrast of the white snow on his navy-blue wool coat, where each flake survived mere seconds before transforming back to water.

Jack was happy to be outside. The bar had begun to feel cloistered and being out in the open allowed him to breathe and to clear his head, at least as much as he could after five drinks in three hours—at least five, Jack wasn't really sure.

Standing in front of the bar, Jack gave himself a mental kick in the ass for not creating a better bar plan, or for that matter, creating one at all. Having hatched the idea of the "Drunk Log" a week before, he hadn't bothered to use the intervening time to map out a personalized pub crawl, instead dwelling mostly on the concept of the log itself. It wasn't that the idea of some sort of directional bar map hadn't occurred to him. He was just acting on the belief that a neighborhood so replete with drinking establishments should pose no challenges when it came to choosing one after another after another. Yet there he stood, the season's first snow falling all around, wondering exactly that—where to next . . .

Jack decided to devise a system, right then and there. So, while the snow continued its less-than-successful attempt to gather on his coat, he coaxed his alcohol infused brain to come up with something coherent. There was no compelling reason for him to do it, but he found the exercise useful, mostly as a way to make his brain work through the effect of the alcohol, which was, quite naturally, having a counterproductive influence on any logical approach to the challenge at hand. Still, he reached the point in his alcohol consumption where an idea didn't really have to be rational; it just needed to *appear* to be rational.

He boldly decided he needed a plan. It didn't really matter if he actually needed one or not, only that he believed he did. So, after a few minutes loitering on the sidewalk, Jack's brain concocted the following:

Whenever he left a bar he would turn left

Then . . . he would walk one block in whatever direction that took him.

Then . . . he would turn right at the end of that block.

Then . . . he would walk two more blocks, if it didn't take him out of the neighborhood.

Then . . . he would go into whatever bar was closest to wherever he was standing.

Needlessly complicated, there was little chance that Jack, despite his native intelligence, would manage to remember all the twists and turns he created for himself after another drink or two—if he could remember any of them at all.

His plan was ridiculous, and Jack was sober enough to know that. *This is ridiculous.*

Smiling at his own idiocy, he turned left to walk the first block, at the end of which he would turn right, should he remember to do so.

It didn't take long for Aria to discover there was little information to be gleaned from the bartender in the pizza joint. She didn't doubt his insistence that he hadn't seen Jack, or even his claim that he didn't know Jack at all. She knew it was more than possible, even probable, that there were bartenders in the neighborhood who didn't know Jack, at least not by name. Luckily, however, she had a selfie of the two of them on her phone, which should spark a memory or two along the way.

Making her task more difficult were the unknowns. It was the things she didn't know that kept Aria planted, at least momentarily, in a bar seat at the pizza place. She came to the conclusion her search method was too random, that if she was going to make any progress, she was going to have to be more methodical. Thus far the search had been characterized by an almost frantic desperation that didn't serve its purpose.

No, she thought, *I need to take a moment and come up with a plan. A real actual plan.*

Aria knew she needed to think of a way to get around the neighborhood that would reduce the chances of missing Jack over and over again, and while she pondered such a plan, Aria had an epiphany. She actually had Jack's phone number. Why she hadn't remembered this over the course of the last hour was beyond her comprehension. She pulled the phone out of the jacket pocket where it had been stashed and found Jack's number.

But what was she going to say? How would she convey her fear to him without sounding like a crazy person? She knew she would have to think on that, as it was crucial to whatever chances she had with him, but she didn't want to wait another moment to act.

The answer dawned on her in a flash. She grabbed her phone and texted.

"Hey!"

It wasn't Hemmingway, she knew, but it was better than nothing. It at least gave her some time to think, which is what Aria did while she waited for Jack to respond. At least she tried to think. Mostly, she just stared at her phone and bounced around a little in her seat, waiting for Jack to answer.

Then, she waited some more.

Then, she decided to extend that.

But no response came.

Aria waited five more excruciating minutes for Jack to text back, and when he didn't, she went ahead and dialed his number, though she still hadn't written her opening lines. If he answered, she would have to improvise.

First ring.

As she listened, Aria mused that she probably hadn't actually called anyone in months. Her preference was to text her friends and family rather than to actually talk to them on the phone using her actual voice and ears. Her mother still used the phone function to call her, however, as if it were the last century, and though Aria had been trying to train her in the ways of modern communication, she still found the sound of a ringing phone too compelling to ignore.

Second ring.

Aria wondered what ring Jack was hearing, if any at all.

Damn phones, she thought. *What are they good for? Absolutely . . .*

Aria realized it might not even be ringing on Jack's end. He might have his phone off. He might be in a place with loud music. There were any number of good reasons why he might not be picking up. Anyway, it was only the second ring. It may be buzzing in his pocket and he just hasn't noticed yet.

Third ring.

Aria took a deep breath, trying to keep frustration at bay. She theorized the ring she was hearing may have actually been the fifth or sixth, that the first few rings on his phone could be undetectable on hers. Or perhaps the reverse. She noticed this odd phone behavior in the past, back when she still used the phone function of her phone.

Fourth ring.

She figured that should be enough. She figured if Jack was going to pick up his damn phone he would have done so already. She feared the possibility that he heard the ring and didn't answer because he didn't recognize the number. Worse still, that he saw her name on the screen and still decided not to answer.

I should hang up.

She tapped her foot on the frame of the bar stool.

I should definitely hang up.

But she didn't. Aria let it ring until it went to voicemail. She left no message. She didn't know what to say.

Jack found another bar, which was no surprise to him. He just wasn't sure the formula had actually gotten him there or if he had stopped short as a result of a failure to follow his own absurd instructions. He suspected the latter. Regardless, he found another bar without really having to think about it and to his credit, he believed, he had found a bar he had yet to patronize in his relatively brief time on the planet.

Cobblestone. Like nearly all the bars in Over-The-Rhine, it was small, so he stood in the snow for a moment, looking through the window to see if he knew anyone inside. He didn't, and that made him happy. He entered and sat at the end of the bar, as far away from the door as possible, but intentionally left the notebook in his pocket. He had learned to wait until he ordered a drink before allowing it to make an appearance, as if it were a traveling companion who might strike up a conversation with a total stranger.

"What can I get for you?"

The bartender was probably close to Jack's age but much scruffier. His quick offer of service had denied Jack the opportunity to put much thought into what he wanted, so he went with what he almost always ordered when he wasn't sure—"The Great Default."

"How about a Black Russian?"

"Hmmm . . ."

The bartender scratched his goatee.

"I don't think I have the ingredients. I don't think I have any cream."

Jack took a deep breath. He had been down this path with Black Russians and bartenders before.

So much for my patented default, except . . .

"Well, that shouldn't be a problem, since there's no cream in a Black Russian."

Jack could feel his teeth clenching and his body tighten. What kind of bartender didn't know how to make a Black Russian?

"Oh, I thought it had cream in it."

The bartender was still rubbing his goatee, either lost in thought or perhaps dealing with a parasitic infection. Jack couldn't be sure but was in no mood to ask.

"No. A *White* Russian has cream in it, but since I ordered a *Black* Russian, we should be okay. That is, as long as you've got vodka and Kahlua. The bar looks pretty well stocked, so I'm willing to bet you've got some vodka and Kahlua back there."

Jack knew he sounded a bit like an ass, but he couldn't help himself. The tape was already rolling and by then he was merely his own audience.

"I'll check."

The bartender, likely annoyed by Jack's condescension, went about his business, turning away from Jack to examine the shelves full of alcohol on the barback. It took only a few seconds for him to locate the requisite ingredients.

"Looks like we've got what you need."

The tenor of his voice had altered in the few moments since Jack sat down. At first affable and welcoming, it was now dry and deadpan.

"Great. I love the things."

Jack was trying to make up for being mean only moments before but was feeling anxious about the bartender's ability to actually make the drink. He decided to share the recipe while trying not to sound like he was sharing the recipe. "Who knew that two shots of vodka and one shot of Kahlua, poured over ice in a rocks glass, could be so tasty? I mean, I don't know how *you* do it, but I usually pour the two shots of vodka first, then add the one shot of Kahlua over the two shots of vodka, because the one shot of Kahlua is heavy, and will sink itself down into the two shots of vodka. Quite simple, really."

The bartender looked at Jack as if he were a professor who had just invited his student to repeat a wobbly thesis.

"I'm on it. Sorry about the mix up with the cream and all that."

It was clear to Jack that the bartender, whose name was Mike, really did want to do the right thing, but as Jack watched him pour the drink, he could tell something was amiss, a hunch proven true by his first sip.

"I'm Mike, by the way."

The bartender watched Jack take his first sip before extending his hand across the bar.

"I'm Jack."

He forced a smile.

"So . . . funny thing . . . this tastes a little different than when I make them."

"Yeah, I hope you like it. I make mine a little softer by using a little less vodka and a little more Kahlua."

Mike was smiling, as if he hadn't heard Jack's instructions at all.

"Ahh . . . I see . . . interesting."

Jack figured this was the best he was going to get out of Mike, that no amount of hint-dropping or outright instruction was going to get him the drink he actually wanted. But there was a light at the end of The Black Russian Tunnel of Hell in which Jack found himself. It was the Drunk Log. He could write all about it in the Drunk Log and Posterity, for ever-ever-after, would know the story of what happened when he tried to order a Black Russian at Cobblestone on that fateful night. It would be his own, private complaint column, and no one would dispute Posterity.

Jack started writing.

Aria didn't move. Jack had not picked up, but the act of calling him had sparked a plan, though it was not without an obvious flaw. She would leave her phone number with the bartenders she met along her way and have them call her if Jack showed up. She would give them a picture as well, so they wouldn't have any problem recognizing him.

It was a good plan, elegant in its simplicity. The flaw involved giving out her phone number to a bunch of random men and women, men and women from whom she didn't want to receive calls for any other reason than to find Jack. The last thing Aria wanted was for her efforts to result in a slew of drunk dials from lonely bar employees, operating under a false assumption that she was even remotely interested in them.

There were definitely a few out there, male and female, with whom she had experienced encounters, nearly none of which bore repeating, though most of them involved nothing more than an innocent, drunken pass. Still, she hadn't come up with anything better when it came to a concrete plan of action. She gave herself a small, mental kick in the ass for not having come up with the plan earlier.

Having settled on a course of action, Aria felt anxious to put it into motion.

"Hey, Tom!"

She called the bartender over and held up the picture of Jack that she had on her phone. "Remember Jack, the guy I asked you about?"

7:14

Stupid fucking bartender. How fucking hard is it to make a drink the right way?

Doesn't he have a cell phone? Doesn't he have access to the internet like everybody else?

Okay, I don't want to get pissy here. Let's just try to enjoy this drink and stay focused.

After all, he didn't completely fuck it up, and I suppose he meant well.

But I just want you to know, Posterity, it appears we might be running out of bartenders who can do anything more than pour a beer or put rum into a glass of Coke.

Maybe we need some on-the-job-training to address situations more challenging than the midnight shift at a college bar.

Maybe we need to start dressing bartenders up in something more professional than cut-off jeans and dirty t-shirts.

Maybe then, and only then, they will decide to take the job seriously.

Wow. I just read that last paragraph and it looks like I actually did get pretty pissy.

Too late now, though. There's no erase button in the log.

You get what you get, even if it's not very good.

If I still had a shrink, she would probably tell me I was acting out.

She'd probably be right, but if I can't direct all this misplaced anger at a stranger

making me the wrong drink, who can I direct it at?

I suppose, if I had my phone, I could vent on YELP.

That might make me feel better. Or maybe it would make me feel meaner.

Well, now that I think about it, I'm glad I left my phone at home.

If I hadn't, I'd be saying my last words on YELP, which is a truly depressing thought.

I've already left enough of my soul on social media.

I didn't need it then and I don't need it now.

Even thinking about it is an interruption I can't afford.

I need to remain focused, well, as much as possible for some-one drinking nonstop.

With a slight shiver, Jack drank about half of what was in the glass. The bar was still fairly empty, and no one seemed to notice him scribbling. The bartender had retreated to the other end of the bar, having no desire to interact further with the cranky man writing in a notebook.

For Jack, the writing seemed to be coming easier than it had when he started at Liberty's. He wasn't sure why, though he suspected it had something to do with repetition and alcohol, both correct assumptions. The looser he got, the easier the words came, even if they didn't always come in the right order or with proper grammar, or if at times his pen didn't keep up with his brain.

Jack thought it a strange phenomenon when his pen fell behind his racing or meandering mind. He had never experienced it before and thought it funny, like watching a movie in which the sound reel is a fraction of a second behind the action on the screen. Every now and again he paused his brain in order to give his pen a chance to catch up. All of this methodology was going through his head as he worked through the less-than-satisfactory Black Russian.

7:22

I have to admit I'm enjoying this, at least in a black comedy sort of way.

I mean, I definitely haven't changed my mind about, you know, about offing myself.

(Sorry, Posterity, you'll have to wait until the end to find out how I'm going to do it.)

I just never thought I would enjoy this part of the process.

I always figured it would be easier just to get plastered and do the deed, but I'm starting to think this was the best part of the plan.

I need you to know, Posterity, that I don't blame anyone else for this. This is all on me.

No one should feel guilty or think they could have stopped it from happening.

Losing Troy was the worst . . .

The worst what, you ask?

I don't think I can put it into words.

It.

Not what happened, but what it meant, what it means right now.

But I think the only way to make this right is to do exactly what I'm doing.

And don't give me all that bullshit about two wrongs don't make a right.

That's what we tell kids when they steal cookies and lie about it.

I have no lies left to tell.

This is real life . . . and death.

Some things you just can't live with . . .

Chapter Eight

Missed Me By This Much

The sound of the door being torn away from the rest of the car was nearly as loud as the accident, or so it seemed to Jack. One of the firemen, Jesse, entered the wreck from the passenger side, looked around the interior, amazed to find a survivor. The dead child, however, broke his heart. This was not his first-time bearing witness to this sort of tragedy, but he had never hardened to it. He could feel the tears welling behind his eyelids. "What's your name sir?" "Jack." The driver was crying also. "We'll get you out of here soon, Jack."

Aria had figured it out. She now understood why she was out in the snow, chasing down a man who was, in fact, really no more than a friendly acquaintance. It had taken her a while to figure it out. Her behavior that night had confused her. When she left Liberty's earlier to follow him, she knew it was the right thing to do; she just didn't know why. She didn't know until that moment outside the pizza place, when the light bulb lit up. In that moment, she recognized it.

It was a feeling she hadn't had for years, which is probably why it took her some time to recognize it. Aria hadn't felt it for more than half a decade, and she couldn't name it back then, either. At least not at first, at least not until her parents found her younger sister in the bathroom.

Her sister, Steffie, had always had problems, or so it seemed. Their mom and dad had her in and out of therapy, hoping she would snap out of whatever funk in which they found her. Sometimes she did just that, and the rest of the nuclear family was gratified and happy that their loved one appeared to be back to normal. Normal for Steffie anyway, if not really "normal" for the most everyone else. As Steffie lurched from emotional crisis to emotional crisis, she dragged her family with her, forcing them to share her pain, anger, or despondence, even if it was something she never really wanted.

Aria and Steffie were close as sisters and as friends, and as the older sister, Aria took responsibility for her sibling's well-being, a task for which she lacked training and understanding.

She never saw her sister's last night coming, never really suspected her baby sister would do herself in. But it was on that night, the night her parents found Steffie, that she came to understand the feeling she had been having for weeks, and she had never forgotten it. The feeling was *dread.*

Jack finished the last of the poorly made Black Russian and debated whether he should give the bartender another chance to make one properly, according to his instructions.

Maybe I am being too harsh, he thought to himself. *Maybe I'm being too judgmental.*

While Jack debated the matter with himself, he glanced out the window at the snow which, by Jack's reckoning, must have been falling steadily for an hour or two, but in reality, had only been falling for thirty or forty minutes, tops. The pavement wasn't yet slick or frozen, but the pace of the snowfall was picking up, allowing it to make some gains. From Jack's perch at the bar, he could no longer see the sidewalk beneath the thin covering of frozen white. In the end, it was the snow that made him to decide to leave Cobblestone. He wanted to be out in the weather, like a child wants to jump in puddles.

7:32

I've decided to leave Cobblestone and not give them a chance to make the drink the right way. Honestly, I think I did every-thing I could to help the guy out, short of hopping over the bar and making it myself, and he still took matters into his own hands.

I might try again at the next bar, or the one after that or after that.

There's plenty of good bartenders out there, as far as I can tell. I just need to find them.

Maybe there's a place where they wear white shirts and tuxedo vests.

Some place I've never been around here.

Fat chance. This is Cincinnati.

I'm pretty sure I can trust someone in a white shirt and a tuxe-do vest to make a good drink.

I feel like if you've taken the time to put on a white shirt and a tuxedo vest, as opposed to a t-shirt, then you've probably al-ready achieved a level of professionalism, which the guy in a t-shirt can only dream of.

Moving on, as I'm sure you are wondering where will I go next. So am I. Let me check.

Jack leafed through the notebook, looking for the instructions he made for himself at Sundry and Vice. It took him less than a minute to realize he hadn't bothered to write them down, at least not in the log. He checked his hands and forearms, but found no words.

7:35

Well, dammit, I can't find those instructions. Did I write them on a napkin? Nope.

They were on a notebook sheet. But what did I do with that?

Jeez, I really don't remember.

That's probably one of the side effects of the five or six drinks I've had so far. Is it five or six?

Six, I think, by now. Maybe.

I keep meaning to go back and count, but I keep forgetting to do that also.

Again, probably because of the drinking.

Duh.

It's fine. I'll wing it.

I think I'm supposed to go left, but I think if I do go left I'll just end up back at Sundry and Vice.

Man, this is turning out to be harder than it should be.

Screw it. I'll wing it.

Jack left cash on the bar, stowed the notebook in his back pocket and ventured once again out into the snow. On a whim, he turned right, rejecting the elaborate plan he had formulated earlier, the same one he couldn't remember. He wasn't at all sure what was supposed to happen after he turned, so he allowed the neighborhood to do the work for him. He had favorites other than Liberty's, so he decided to let his feet do the talking and lead him where they may. *Hopefully, to a good Black Russian,* he thought.

Aria was still feeling proud of herself as she turned north to go back up Main Street until, at least, she discovered the second flaw in her plan.

When she initially started looking for Jack, she hadn't yet thought to give out her phone number or show the picture of Jack. Now, she was going to have to go back to places she had already been, the places she *hadn't* shown the picture. However, despite having to retrace some steps, a couple benefits occurred to her. The first was that, since she had begun her search, some of the bartenders' shifts had ended and new ones had arrived, and Jack may have retraced his steps as well, though she had no reason to think so. Just hope. The other was that she would no longer need to search randomly through the neighborhood. She could use the street grid to her advantage. As soon as she hit every place going north on Main, she could just pop over to Walnut, go south and hit every bar on that street, and then north again on Vine, etc., until she covered every street in Over-the-Rhine.

Genius, she told herself.

Aria's trepidation about randomly handing out her phone number lessened each time she did it. She figured, should one of the recipients choose to take liberties with her number, she could always block theirs and that would be that. She took note that some of the bartenders were more open than others about receiving the instructions and information she was attempting to disperse. So, if one of them seemed distant or distracted, she would just order a drink and engage them when they brought the drink to her.

The male bartenders were easy. All she had to do was touch their hand and stare into their eyes while she explained what she was up to. This worked on a couple of the female bartenders as well, but she felt lucky she didn't have to buy more than a few drinks along the way. It wasn't that she couldn't drink. She could. It was that she wanted to keep her wits about her while on the hunt, so even if she had to order a drink, she didn't always finish it, and she made sure to order something inexpensive. She wasn't made of money, after all.

Mark E. Scott

Before long, Aria ended up back at Liberty's, which had gotten busier since she left nearly an hour earlier. The snow had not been a hindrance, at least not until she reached the sidewalk in front of the bar, the part on which the three pink pigs resided. The three stout, cast-iron pigs occupied space in front of Liberty's, their piggy feet cemented into the sidewalk, because at some point in its history the bar had been owned by three police officers who thought it would be humorous to embrace the negative moniker for their profession as an actual, physical manifestation. The pigs served as an object of interest for the uninitiated, a rally point for Liberty's first timers, and as an outdoor seating area for smokers. On occasion, the pigs had been defaced by graffiti "artists," but their work rarely lasted more than a few hours, as the current owners kept a can of pink paint handy at all times.

It was in front of these pigs that Aria took the first of three falls that evening. In this instance, her unintended descent to the pigs and pavement was caused by a regular, happy to see Aria outside the bar, where he was smoking and talking with friends. The friendly patron went in for a hug, losing his footing on the now snowy pavement just as his outstretched arms were reaching his favorite bartender. Before he knew what was happening, his feet were off the ground. A casual observer might have described his movement as akin to sliding into second base. Unfortunately for Aria, her role in this little bit of physical comedy was second baseman, and she came down hard over the legs of the would-be hugger, her head glancing ever-so-slightly off one of the pig's snouts, but with enough force to raise a welt on her left cheek bone. The somewhat inebriated base runner was, of course, terribly apologetic and joined the throng now assisting Aria on the short journey into the bar, where a bag of ice was speedily created and applied by her co-worker, Aaron.

94

For her part, Aria felt no animosity toward her friendly attacker, nor did she take the fall as a sign that she should abbreviate her search for Jack. Instead, she viewed the whole event as a problem to be overcome, and after the few minutes it took for the welt to recede, and after asking about Jack, Aria was back on the street, on her way to Walnut, where she would work her way south, giving out her phone number and a picture of Jack to any bartender willing to take them.

Jack's right turn sent him east, back in the direction of Main, where Liberty's was situated and where his entire evening had started. He knew he wasn't going to return to Liberty's. He had no intention of visiting any place twice, not on this particular evening. That part of the plan he remembered. As well, Liberty's was located on the north end of the street, making it easier to avoid. He would connect with Main nearly three blocks south. So, while he might get close to Liberty's, he wouldn't get close enough for it to tempt him. This was what was on Jack's mind while he stood in the snow, waiting for the light to change at 12th and Vine.

But Jack couldn't help feeling drawn to Liberty's. He had an urge to see Aria before the end of the night, before the end of him. She was the reason he wanted to return to where he started, though he believed it a bad idea.

Without much fanfare, there had grown in him a sneaking realization that Aria had begun to represent something special to him, something he recognized she could never be.

Hope.

Hope that things would get better.

Hope that he could be cleansed of his sins.

Jack was right about this, of course, because whatever he wanted Aria to be would be something unfair, something for which she did not bargain. It would be something in which she had yet to have a say. She couldn't be his lifeline.

He had no right to do that to her.

He tried to forget about it.

Jack was enjoying his time in the snow despite the potential water damage to the log, which he kept snug in his back pocket, where it was safe and dry under the protective umbrella of his wool coat. Still, his hand kept reflexively checking to make sure it was still there, that it hadn't fallen out somewhere between Cobblestone and wherever he was meandering. To anyone who cared to notice, it looked as if Jack couldn't stop grabbing his right butt cheek, like he had a nervous tick. But the behavior had ingrained itself and Jack didn't notice.

Jackson Street was a block before Walnut. Just two blocks long, it contained the Cincinnati Art Academy on one side of 12th and the Know Theatre on the other. It was the Know that caught Jack's attention as he crossed over Jackson. Besides the fringe and experimental shows they usually presented, the Know also had a bar, which would be very quiet if a play was running.

Jack was in a mood to write, and the theater was only a few steps away, but when he reached the door, he found there was no play that evening, which meant the bar was closed.

In consolation, Jack took a seat at one of the two picnic tables in front of the building, protected from the falling snow by an overhang, and decided this was the perfect opportunity to be left alone, utterly and completely. There were no other bars or restaurants on Jackson. Foot traffic on a Friday night would be almost non-existent.

7:46

I'm sitting at a picnic table in front of the Know Theatre on a Friday night.

96

I feel like a derelict, out of step, but at least I'm alone.

Here's something interesting, Posterity, or I hope you find it interesting.

Now, before you read this next part, make sure there's no children around.

Ha! Hold on a minute. For all I know YOU are a child.

I mean, I can't control what happens to this after I give it up.

Literally, anyone who finds it could read it.

Well, then, let me think about this a moment.

If you ARE a child, then maybe I shouldn't tell you this next part.

But how can you be a child, Posterity?

In my head, you're sort of a representation of everything that's ever happened and,

if that's the case, then nothing I say is going to surprise you. You've seen it all, so to speak.

But if that's true, then I feel like what I'm about to say is actually really innocent, and boring.

But what the hell—here goes: I lost my virginity to Susan Ballard.

Okay, I know on the surface this is pretty basic stuff. But there's more.

She had a broken leg, and it was our first date.

I was driving an old Pontiac (remember those) and I had to put her leg,

the one with the cast, up on the dashboard and maneuver around her.

It was all over so quick, I felt like a dumbass.

She gave me a second chance, though, after we went to a pizza place for dinner

(that's right, we didn't make it to dinner until AFTER.)
Second time was 100% better, or that's how I remember it, anyway.
We never really dated after that. Just the occasional . . . you know . . .
Not sure why all this came up, Posterity.
So basic. So simple.
So much has happened since then.
Some of it is worth remembering, like Susan . . . and the Pontiac.
Most of it isn't.

The snow was falling harder, infiltrating Jack's spot at the picnic table under the overhang. When the first flake hit the log, he folded it up and shoved it back down into his pocket. It was time to go. The cold from the wooden bench had begun working its way into Jack's pants and was threatening to go further.

As he stood and stretched, Jack decided to go to Japp's. There wasn't a drink the Japp's bartenders didn't know how to make. With the log safely in his back pocket, and being careful not to slip in the snow, Jack left what was a perfect spot just moments ago and headed to Japp's, maybe a hundred yards away. He could see the sign once he turned the corner. He could see the front door as it came into view. Indeed, the close proximity, combined with Jack's belief he could order a drink without having to explain it to the person who was supposed to know how to make it, brought him a sense of renewed calm. Just a block and a half separated him from that nirvana, and the only obstacles between him and Japp's were two cross walks and a dog taking a dump on the sidewalk.

Dodging the dog was not a problem, though as he skirted around the otherwise stationary house pet, Jack noted the poor thing appeared to be a tad constipated, or so it seemed. The retriever was squatting when Jack came into its view and was still squatting after Jack carefully scooched around him. Out of brotherhood and common courtesy, he wanted to give the dog his space. Certainly, Jack didn't like being disturbed when engaged in similar activities.

Now just a block away from Japp's and what was sure to be a perfect Black Russian, Jack waited for the light to change so that he could make it safely across the first cross walk. He had no interest in getting mowed down by a driver paying more attention to the phone in their lap than to the sea of humanity through which they were wading in his or her deadly steel chariot.   But Jack's attention to the traffic in the busy intersection was misplaced. He was not in any danger of getting run over by a full-size vehicle. No. That's because it turned out the thing to which he should have been paying attention was a rental scooter with a moron for a driver.

The moron, whose name was Patrick, thought it would be fun to ride in the snow. But he also thought it too dangerous to ride the scooter in the street on a busy Friday night, though the law and the agreement he signed before activating the scooter both indicated otherwise. Not to mention, this was Patrick's first time on a scooter, drunk or not. Despite his lack of experience, Patrick only gave the instructions a cursory reading.

Moments later, Patrick hopped on the two-wheeled machine, ready to take on the world, or at least a piece of it, just two blocks from the intersection where Jack was waiting for the light to change.

Patrick's scooter journey, like that of so many before him, proved to be short but eventful. Initially he demonstrated the wherewithal to notice the dog trying to poop on the sidewalk, the same one Jack had encountered moments before, and somehow manage to avoid the retriever. But after scrupulously guiding the scooter around the stationary pup, things began to go awry. Patrick, for reasons he didn't fully understand, began to accelerate, and by the time he turned his attention away from the retriever back to the snow-covered sidewalk, it was too late. Jack, and two or three other unsuspecting pedestrians, were only feet away, right in Patrick's kill zone. Too close, it turned out, for a less-than-sober Patrick to attempt any course correction that might have helped him avoid mowing down one of his fellow citizens.

The hit was sufficient to knock Jack flat, face down in the street. Though he couldn't immediately know it, Jack's consolation for taking one for the team was that the force of the collision was sufficient to eject Patrick from the scooter, sending him flying over the handlebars onto his back, smack in the middle of the crosswalk.

For his malfeasance, Patrick received a cracked skull and severe concussion, as well as a fine from the city. For Jack, however, the fates intervened. Against all odds, he walked away, virtually unscathed.

"Are you alright?"

A young man named Lamar, who had been lucky enough to be standing a foot to Jack's left, stepped into the street to render him assistance. Lamar felt no compunction to check on Patrick who, in this case, was a victim only of his own poor judgement.

Jack rolled over and looked up at Lamar, taking a deep breath before he spoke.

"You know what, I think I'm okay."

Lamar helped him to his feet.

"Then you must have a guardian angel. You went down hard. It looked really ugly from where I was standing."

"You're telling me! But I think you're the one with the guardian angel. Could have been you." Jack took another deep breath and gave himself a once over.

"You know, I'm good. Crazy as that sounds, I'm good."

"Well, alright then. I hope the rest of your night goes better."

Jack shook Lamar's hand, gave him a pat on the back, and went on his way, walking past the prone figure of Patrick, who hadn't moved a muscle since he landed.

The spectacle attracted a crowd, which quickly formed around the victim and his assailant. Initially the gawkers assumed Patrick dead which, if true, would make for a great bar story later in the evening. It was only after he began to move, followed soon after by a proof-of-life groan, that the crowd, perhaps not without just a touch of disappointment, learned he had survived. As soon as an ambulance arrived, nearly everyone vanished, including Jack, who was making a beeline, or something resembling a beeline, to Japp's.

Chapter Nine

Stumbling in the Snow

It was easy enough for the firemen to remove the passenger door, but once they were able to see inside, they realized they wouldn't be able to get the man or the boy out through that side of the vehicle. The boy's body was compressed between the steering wheel and the man's torso, and Jesse knew he was already dead. They were going to have to remove the driver's door and the steering wheel. To Jesse, the man looked like he was going to black out. "Jack? Can you hear me, Jack?" The man nodded. "Listen Jack, we can't get you out this way. We have to take your door off. Do you understand?" The man nodded again.

Aria worked her way down Walnut. It didn't take her long. There were far fewer bars on Walnut than on Vine or Main. She left her information in 16 Bit, a bar with gobs of 1980's video games that could be played for free by patrons and thought that would be it until she got to the corner of 12th and Walnut. She was therefore surprised when she came across Homemaker's which, unbeknownst to her, had just recently opened. Aria thought she knew every place in the neighborhood.

As she approached the intersection and was about to duck inside, Aria noticed a crowd of people hovering around the corner. Something told her she should walk over and find out what was going on, but she reminded herself that 12th and Walnut was always busy on Friday nights, and so she didn't give it a second thought.

Aria didn't recognize either of the female bartenders inside Homemaker's, but a red flag went up as soon as she saw a man her age, sitting at the bar, alone. Bill. His presence was almost enough to send her scurrying back out into the street. She had broken up with him a year-and-a- half ago and it hadn't been pretty. In fact, she still suspected him of stealing her passport and keying her car in two separate acts of revenge. Although Bill never confessed to either transgression, she had to admit that she hadn't put much effort into getting him to fess up.

For her, the missing passport and scratched paint were a small price to pay for her personal freedom. It wasn't that Bill was a bad guy. He was just bad for Aria, and now here she was, faced with the prospect of talking to him after nearly eighteen months of no communication. She dreaded whatever words might come out of his mouth, or hers, for that matter. Her knee-jerk strategy was to pretend she didn't see him sitting there, and so she soldiered on to the bar to continue her self-appointed mission.

While Patrick received offers of assistance from people who had witnessed what a local journalist later called "assault-by-scooter," Jack continued on his way, rolling Lamar's words over in his head.

Do I have a guardian angel?

He supposed it was possible, though the thought of it brought a se-vere pang of guilt. *What made me deserving? Why not Troy?*

Jack knew he was extremely lucky. He had avoided a much more serious outcome and would not be written about as the main collateral damage of Patrick's runaway scooter. No one is interested in someone who did not receive even a scratch. Still, as he glanced back at the sight of the debacle, Jack believed the man sprawled on the icy ground was surely in need of the ambulance that had just arrived.

Jack heard more sirens coming closer and assumed the police were coming to see what they could determine about Patrick and the Friday night massacre he nearly caused. Then again, Jack thought that it quite possible the sirens were intended for something completely different, like a robbery or some sort of dust-up between rival illegal drug vendors. Regardless, he had no desire to wait around and answer questions from paramedics or cops. He didn't have time and, besides, even if he had suffered an injury from the collision, any consequences would soon be rendered irrelevant.

I got a plan and I'm sticking to it.

Jack, forgiving by virtue of his own experience, had no desire to inflict any additional justice on the scooter driver, Patrick, who had definitely taken the worst of the hit and would be paying for it for days, if not weeks or months. So, instead of hanging around, waiting for more authorities to arrive, Jack kept moving, determined to get to Japps, no matter what or who may try to interfere.

Bill, apparently, was not going to allow Aria to ignore him. She felt a tap on her shoulder right after she walked up to the bar at Homemaker's.

"Aria, are you going to say hello?"

Despite the valiant attempt, Aria had not held out much hope that her cloak of emotional invisibility would really work. She was forced to acquiesce.

"Hi, Bill. How's it going?"

She really didn't know what else to say to him. More so, she didn't *want* to say anything, to him or anyone else, unless it was to inquire about Jack. She hadn't seen him in months, and she liked it that way. Bill, however, being the insensitive boob he had always been, failed to pick up on her reticence to engage him in conversation. She wasn't surprised. His inability to gauge her mood was one of the many failings she noted before and after breaking up with him.

"Good, good. It's been a while, hasn't it? Are you here alone?"

Aria was only slightly surprised he was coming on to her.

Just part of his irresistible charm, I guess.

As she stood there, waiting for Bill to either go away or for a trap door to suddenly suck her (alone) into a black hole, Aria wondered again why she ever dated him in the first place. Probably his body, she thought. He always had a good body.

"Yup, I am. Here. Alone. But not for long. I just need to talk to the bartender for a minute and then I'm leaving."

Aria was doing a good job of speaking to Bill while *not* looking directly at him, naively hoping he would finally get that she had no interest in carrying on a conversation, let alone take him home for a quickie—for old time's sake.

Mercifully, one of the bartenders arrived to take Aria's drink order before Bill had a chance to respond. It also gave her the opportunity to ignore him while she engaged the bartender in her search for Jack. The bartender promised she would share the information with her coworker and let Aria know if they saw Jack.

Once her mission was complete, and she had thanked the bartender for being so willing to help, Aria no longer had an obvious reason to ignore Bill.

"Looking for a guy?"

Bill smiled.

"Yes, Bill, I'm looking for a guy. And it's really none of your business."

Aria tried her best to demonstrate her frustration. She just wanted to get out.

"There's one right here in front of you, Aria."

Bill sensed he was running out of time and decided to throw the Hail Mary, which to no one's surprise, including Bill's, did not work.

"Whatever, Bill. I'm out."

Aria packed her phone into her purse, turned on her heel and walked out of the bar, happy to be done with the episode.

Walking out into the snow and looking down Walnut, Aria could see the crowd on the corner had dispersed somewhat, but she noted there was now an ambulance and a police car, lights flashing, blocking one of the lanes. Intrigued, she picked up her step, covering the distance quickly, and mixing herself in with the crowd enjoying the light show.

"Jeez. What the hell is going on?"

Aria was speaking to a girl next to her. From where they were standing, she could see Patrick (although she didn't know his name was Patrick) laying on a stretcher, mumbling to two policemen as the paramedics got him ready to load into the ambulance.

"I wasn't here but somebody told me that guy on the stretcher over there was flying down the sidewalk on a scooter and he ran into a guy that was standing on the corner. I guess the scooter-guy went head over heels and ended up in the middle of the street. I wish I had been there to see it. I'll bet it was amazing."

The girl was clearly disappointed, perhaps hoping to see an abundant mix of blood in the snow or to hear mournful, funereal music being played by a band in the background.

"Wow!"

Aria shared the informant's desire to have seen the wreck, minus the blood and the band, and her disappointment at having missed it. After all, how often does one get the chance to watch someone fly over the handlebars of a scooter, or the handlebars of anything, for that matter.

"What happened to the other guy?"

"Who?"

"The one who got hit?"

"I guess he just got up and walked away. He was gone by the time I got here. They said he didn't seem to be hurt, even though he got flattened by the scooter-guy and seemed kind of dazed when he walked away."

"Tough guy, maybe."

"Or maybe he was too shitfaced to feel anything."

Aria contemplated the idea of just walking away right after getting nailed by an electric scooter and decided she had seen everything there was to see—for the moment. Had she looked down 12th Street, she might have seen Jack ducking into Japp's. Instead, she wound her way through the crowd to get to the last bar on Walnut before heading east to Vine.

Every Friday night, Japp's hosted a jazz band, which was quite popular with the Happy Hour crowd. Having finished playing just before Jack arrived, he saw them packing their instruments as he walked through the front door. For this, Jack was happy. The departure of the jazz band, along with their fans, meant the place would be quiet for a while, though he wasn't sure for how long. Jack had never actually been in Japps on a Friday *after* the jazz band departed, at least not for very long. Though he was sure they were open until at least one or two in the morning, he wasn't at all sure what transpired post-jazz-band on a Friday night.

The interior of Japp's, like most of the old buildings, was set up in shotgun formation. The long bar ran nearly the length of one side of the narrow room, and a line of tables occupied the wall opposite. The tables were nearly abandoned, and he grabbed the one furthest from the door, in what looked to be a discrete corner. The walls surrounded the table on two sides, preventing anyone from sneaking up on him. Jack still needed a drink, however, so he laid his coat across the chair in order to claim it, just in case there was another one of him, looking for a table all by themselves in a semi-dark corner of a bar on a cloudy Friday night with the snow falling outside.

It's like I just escaped something and need a drink . . .

"What can I get for you, Jack?"

Denny the bartender was prompt, almost as if he had been waiting for Jack to walk over.

"Black Russian, please."

"Good choice. Absolut okay for the vodka?"

Denny's obvious control over the Black Russian situation brought Jack a sense of calm.

"I'll leave that to you, Denny."

The bartender smiled and took less than a minute to make the drink. Jack took it back to his corner table and started writing.

8:01

Jeez! Can you believe what just happened?

That guy could have killed me.

Hmmm, I think I just discovered the meaning of irony. Maybe not. I don't know though.

Maybe it would have been better had he done my job for me. Maybe not.

He'd probably have felt guilty about it. If he lives.

Anyway, he seemed to take the lion's share of the damage.

I can't stand those scooters on the sidewalk.

But I'm feeling pretty good, especially for a guy who just got run over.

I guess when I say I feel pretty good I don't mean just physically.

I'm feeling . . . content?

I read somewhere that once somebody really decides to off themselves, they actually get happy.

*They, meaning head-shrinkers, think it's because they know
that whatever's been bothering them, whatever pain they're in,
and have been for quite some time, will be gone soon.
I think that's me. I am feeling sort of peaceful now.
At least more than I did earlier, or yesterday, or a week ago.
Or a month ago.
Who knows? Maybe I'm just drunk enough not to care any-
more.
Either way it's okay, Posterity. You need to know I'll be okay
and I am. I'm okay.*

As Jack took a sip of the Black Russian, he considered it to be the
best one he had ever consumed. He would make sure to leave a tip that
properly expressed his thanks for getting the drink right. Had Denny
asked if he wanted Coke in the Black Russian, he thought, he might have
killed him before he had the chance to kill himself.

*That kind of violation merits violence. Thank God we've avoided
that.*

Jack looked down at his words and felt a vague sadness. What he
was feeling now was nothing compared to the intensity of despair he felt
after killing his nephew, and he let it wash over and through him without
much effort. Indeed, Jack noted, in the breadth of time since the accident, nearly all of life's little problems had come to seem trivial, even
almost getting killed by Patrick the Moron, and by that night, they were
barely registering as anything Jack felt compelled to deal with or even
remotely remember.

But what about Aria?

Jack took another long sip of his drink and picked up his log to write.

8:11

I want you to know, considering how my evening is going to end,

that I really don't have any "affairs" to put in order.

That will make it easier for you, Posterity.

There is no house to sell or car payments to take care of. No property owned.

I rent an apartment and I paid off my car years ago.

Oh—something you should know. I left my will in a safe deposit box.

Dad has the spare key so he shouldn't have any problem getting in.

You'll just want to grab everything out of there before they know I'm dead.

I mean, before the bank knows I'm dead.

They don't like to let living people into dead people's safe deposit boxes.

Things get complicated after that, apparently.

There are some pictures of Troy and me in there. Charlie and Sarah may want those.

I don't think they ever saw those ones.

Everything's on phones and computers, but I had those printed. Just wanted to make those moments permanent.

By the way, I'm at Japp's now and having a Black Russian, made the way God intended.

If I am left alone by the masses, I might break my rule again and stay here for another.

I'm sitting at this quiet table in the corner. Everyone's leaving me alone.

Fingers crossed it doesn't get busy. The bartender probably feels differently.
I'm exhausted.

After leaving the crime scene without delving any further into the facts of the case, Aria continued south to Central Parkway, one of the widest streets downtown and under which exists never-used subway tunnels from the 1920's. Aria did not know the full story of the rise and fall of the Cincinnati subway system, but she knew the tunnels had been dug and the stations built. No cars, though. She remembered reading somewhere that the main reason for its demise was because the project ran out of money just before they were ready to actually buy the subway cars, but someone told her that was wrong. She had never taken the time to really find out, and now, for some reason, she regretted it.

If only I knew that stuff, I would really be in demand at parties.

She was sure, however, that what were now abandoned subway tunnels were once the Miami-Erie canal, which, having been drained, provided a convenient hole to be transformed into a subway. Aria had never been much of a history buff, but as she stood on the sidewalk in the snow, she felt a touch of remorse for the death of the Cincinnati subway. Not just because there were many occasions where she could have been comfortably underground, waiting for a train, instead of outside in the weather, as she was now.

Ever-so-slightly, she mourned what could have been. What would her city have become had its subway been completed when it had its best chance to do so? She let go of the thought as fast as she could. She would not allow herself to entertain any ideas of an empty subway tunnel as a metaphor for her own life, as much as an empty tunnel could be, anyway.

Not going there. Nope.

A dog yip disturbed Aria's meditation. In the middle of Central, on the grassy median strip, a Yorkshire Terrier was doing his business. The grass on the strip was now covered in white, and it appeared the dog was enjoying the first real snowfall of the year, although it may have been complaining, given the proximity of its privates to the cold snow underneath it.

Aria wasn't sure how long the two of them had been out there, but judging from the behavior of the lady holding the leash, it appeared to have already been too long. She was bundled against the brisk wind now whipping the snow, and Aria could hear her imploring the dog to take action and do its thing. The wide street provided no opposition to the blowing flakes, which had made Aria their target as well. She missed the shelter of the buildings behind her, so she got moving, silently hoping for the sake of dog and owner that the small creature would mercifully poop in short order.

Because of the wind, Aria didn't walk the extra block to Vine Street. Instead, she turned right on Jackson and back into the protection of the buildings lining each side of the narrow street. Like Jack earlier, she knew the only bar on Jackson was inside the Know Theater. She suspected it wouldn't be open and she was correct, but just to make sure she slid through the snowy picnic tables, one of which, unseen by her, still sported an imprint of Jack's ass. She peaked through the window. Sure enough, there was no activity on the other side of the glass. She worked her way back out from between the tables and headed to Vine, silently counting the number of bars she would find there. She found the number a tad staggering. In the space of four blocks, she figured there were at least sixteen bars or restaurants with bars in them, and those were just the ones she could list in her head. She knew, most likely, that she missed a few.

The damn things were popping up all the time.

Jack was still sitting by himself. Fifteen minutes after his arrival, he was still sitting alone. He couldn't believe it. He felt exceedingly pleased by this stroke of luck and, since he found the corner so peaceful, made the command decision to have an additional, hassle-free Black Russian. Jack was getting quite comfortable with the idea of breaking his one-drink-per-bar rule again, which regardless had only been loosely enforced. Jack was so engrossed in his calculations he nearly failed to take note of the DJ carrying his gear into the bar, walking right by Jack to set up in the back of the room. When this did register, he was not pleased.

"Uh, what's going on here?"

Denny the bartender was making a drink for someone else but didn't miss a beat.

"You mean the DJ? We have a DJ in here on Friday nights, after the jazz."

"What kind of music?"

"Oh, you know, dance stuff. I think he does old school stuff, though, like the B52's. That sort of thing."

The news shattered Jack's vision of peace.

"How long do I have?"

The bartender looked non-plussed for a second, as if Jack had hit him with a real existential doozy. Then, he thought better of it.

"You mean, how long until he starts?"

Jack nodded.

"I don't know. Pretty soon after he gets set up, generally."

Jack returned to his beautiful corner and pulled the log out his back pocket. Taking a deep breath, he was almost able to convince himself his panic was misplaced. The place was still empty, he had half his drink, and it would be at least ten or twenty minutes before the DJ would be ready to play.

He set pen to paper.

Chapter Ten

More Water, Please

Now the grinding sound was right next to him. He and the boy were under some sort of blanket. Jack barely remembered the fireman pulling it over them, telling him it was to protect them from the sparks. Under the blanket, Jack felt he was drowning, buried. He was trapped under the blanket with Troy. He was trapped under the blanket. His thoughts got drowned out by the sound of the door being torn away from the rest of the car.

8:17
When Troy was born.
When Troy was born . . .
When Troy was born, I had just gotten my engineering degree.
Before that, I was just another dumbass college student.
My brother, Charlie, graduated a couple years before and married Sarah, the girl of his dreams, I was best man. Maybe I wasn't, but I was.
And right after that, I disappeared.
They got a house. I helped them move their crap but that was about it.
I left as soon as the last box was out of the truck.
Why did I disappear? I'm not sure.
I've thought about it for years. I used to think it was because I had my own things to do.

I was just starting a new job and needed to focus. That sort of thing.

It's all bullshit. I was just being a prick.

I didn't know where I fit in to Charlie's life anymore, so I skipped out. It was a dick move.

Then, about a year after the marriage, Troy was born.

Not sure why they decided to have a kid so quickly, but I figured they must have been going at it like rabbits, and Troy just happened.

Didn't matter, though.

They were super-happy, and I started getting into it, too.

They started calling me Uncle Jack and sending me those pictures,

the ones where the baby looks like a submarine on a sonar.

The whole family was excited, really.

Troy was the first grandchild for Mom and Dad and for Sarah's parents, too.

Troy got everybody together before he was even born.

Things started slow with us.

Early on, Charlie and Sarah didn't need me to do much to help out.

One set of grandparents always seemed ready to babysit, if they needed it.

I mean, I'd go over and see him, but babies don't do much.

Lay there, mostly. Eat, pee, poop, and cry. That's about it.

But everybody goes crazy over them anyway, as if they're little Einsteins,

crapping their diapers. Like clockwork.

And I'll admit, I gave up on the diaper changes the first time he peed in my mouth.

Learned a lesson that day. Cover that thing up!

Things really started to change for us when he was three or four.

He could talk and walk and cause trouble.

Honestly, I think most of being a parent is just keeping kids alive.

If you can do that, you're ahead of the game.

But the great thing about Troy (okay here it is)

When he was that age, we already had the same sense of humor.

We both thought farts were funny, and any video of a guy getting hit in the nuts.

Who knew toddlers were so adult?

The more we hung out the more we liked each other,

although I'm not sure he was a very good judge of character.

He always wanted to give money to panhandlers, which I took as a sign of naivete'.

Still, we kinda fell in love with each other, and yeah, that's what happened.

We reached a point where I'd just pick him up from Charlie and Sarah,

whether they needed a sitter or not.

I think I was really useful after they had Danielle.

Getting Troy out of the house worked for everybody.

We spent a lot of time at the zoo and the aquarium but, really, any place would do.

Oh, and the kid was a chick magnet. I'd get smiles from women whenever we were out.

It was more than all that, of course. I actually just enjoyed being around him.

He was more fun than half of my friends. And smart, too, at
least in a dumb-kid way.
Besides farts and ball-shots we also shared a love of root beer,
ice cream, and baseball.
We must have gone to dozens of Reds games,
and he only threw up once from too much ice cream.
I blamed the heat. After that, I made sure we always had seats
in the shade.
We never told Charlie and Sarah about it.
It was a secret. It was one of our secrets.
We had many.
That last day, the day I killed him, we spent at the Children's
Museum.
His favorite thing was the rope bridges strung across the fake
treetops.
They were suspended fifteen or twenty feet off the floor,
and Troy always wanted me up there with him.
I offered, more than once, to let him bring one of his school
friends,
you know, somebody his own age,
but he said no.
He just wanted me.
Looking back, I suppose it's a good thing nobody else was in
the car,
but I'm glad he had a good last day.
We had ice cream before we left.

Jack put the pen down and closed the notebook. He didn't want to
cry in a bar. He didn't want to cry at all. Ever. *There's already been*
enough of that, he thought, *and it hadn't made a difference.* It wouldn't

117

make a difference now. Reliving it for the umpteenth time wouldn't change anything.

Japp's was still empty and Jack was still alone. He finished his drink without really noticing and had yet to decide whether to have another or move on. It was quite a dilemma, but one for which he was happy. It took his mind off Troy.

To drink or not to drink more than one in the same bar.

Jack made a quick attempt to measure his level of drunkenness, the very act of which, at least to him, an indication he wasn't too drunk, not for him anyway, at least not on that night. If he was too drunk, he reasoned, he wouldn't at all care about how drunk he might be. The self-assessment, however, did clue Jack into the fact that he was, if not hammered, then at least pretty buzzy, so he decided to give himself a drunk test, which really just involved walking a straight line to the bathroom. This, with the help of the bar rail, he managed to do, and was even successful at dodging another patron in order to avoid a human-to-human collision in front of the restroom. Jack did not count the incident against himself in the walking-straight test and, once safely peeing in the urinal, assigned himself a grade of "A." *Aced it,* he told himself.

Aria didn't have far to walk before the plethora of bars on Vine presented themselves. Once past the empty theater, the first bar on her self-inflicted agenda was only a block away. She walked along 12th in the snow, using the parking garage on her left as a wind break, thinking ahead on the task she had set for herself.

I'm finding him. That's all there is to it.

By that time, by the time she was hugging the side of the parking garage for protection, she had stopped wondering why she was out in the snow, looking for a man to whom she owed nothing, her resolve strengthened by an inner voice, telling her she was doing the right thing.

She had been hearing the inner voice for years and, to the best of her knowledge, it had never led her astray, especially on those occasions when she chose to actually listen to it. Indeed, Aria's inner voice was something on which she'd learned to rely in the quarter century since being expelled from her mother's womb. She learned to trust its ability to alert her to things she might otherwise have overlooked.

Most recently, her inner voice intervened on her behalf just a month before. She was thinking about getting a puppy. Feeling alone, she thought of ways to cure her loneliness, coming to the conclusion that bringing a four-legged creature into her life and apartment would relieve the loneliness.

The inner voice, which Aria had never named but had, for no obvious reason, always associated with her grandmother, told her it was a bad idea. The voice told Aria that her schedule barely left her enough time to bathe, let alone take care of a doggie that would wake her up early every morning, begging to be taken outside, and which would likely pee all over the place. Aria listened to the voice, and got a cat instead, an alternative to which the voice offered no protest. She named the cat Stella, after her grandmother.

When Aria reached Vine, she almost took a pass on the first place that came into her field of vision. It was another restaurant with a bar in it, an empty one as far as she could tell, and by Jack's own accounting he almost never spent any time in restaurant bars. Despite her determination to be thorough in her search, the foul weather made Aria keen on efficiency and skipping bars with a low probability of a Jack sighting was one way she could move the process along. She decided, however, that she couldn't risk it and went in anyway.

You just never know.

It may or may not have been true, but by the time Aria was back out on the street she would have sworn the snow was coming down harder

119

than it had all evening. Whatever heat had been stored by the daytime sun in the sidewalk cement appeared to have been spent and the snow was now clearly winning the battle for dominance over the walkways, if not yet the streets. The cars and the heat of their engines had thus far left the street mostly visible, but the sidewalks had begun to disappear altogether. Aria was pleased with herself. In anticipation of the snow, she had worn her hiking boots to work that evening. The voice had been right again.

Jack swooned, standing at the bar, contemplating his next move. He wasn't sure if he stood up too fast, or if the alcohol started seeping through the layers of adrenaline and distraction he had inadvertently constructed throughout the evening. It wasn't that he didn't enjoy the swoon, so much as he was afraid of losing his footing, which he found to be ironic, like a mountain goat with vertigo. After all, he had been flattened by a scooter and lived to tell the tale. But there he was, swooning. Jack grabbed the edge of the bar to steady himself and waited for the bartender, who arrived poste-haste.

"More water, please."

"Is that it? Is that all you need?"

Jack wondered at the question, or at least the way it was asked.

"How come you seem weird?"

To Jack, Denny the bartender appeared to be floating behind the bar. Denny was still staring.

"Jack, are you alright? You don't look so good."

Jack stared back blankly. He wanted to take a nap.

"Whad'ya mean?"

"Dude, you're all pale and look like you're going to fall over. Jack, you should go check yourself out in the bathroom."

Jack intended to take the bartender's advice, and even managed to start working his way to the end of the bar, holding its edge the entire trip. Upon reaching the terminus of the bar and, by default, the end of his stabilizer, he panicked just a little, realizing he did not have the where-withal to go any further without additional assistance.

"This must be what it's like to be old."

Jack spoke to no one in particular and wasn't sure if anyone could hear him.

"Is it?"

The bartender, like Jack, had come to the conclusion his patron wasn't going to make it to the water closet on his own and rushed around the bar to render assistance, helping him to a couch in the back room, carefully depositing him on the smooth, cool leather.

"I'll get you that water now, Jack. Do you want me to call anybody?"

The question perturbed Jack. He didn't need anybody to call any-body. He was just fine. He tried to keep the perturbation out of his voice when he responded to the offer of assistance.

"Fuck no."

Denny shrugged. He'd heard it all before and was thankful that he'd made it this far with Jack without being thrown up on, spat upon, or slapped.

It was in that moment Jack decided he was going to have to leave Japp's. The bar had not yet begun to refill, and the lack of customers gave Denny ample time to hover around, attempting to render assistance to any stray drinker. Jack found this situation unacceptable. For his part, the bartender brought Jack a full glass of water, standing over him until he decided that Jack required no additional aid. Jack was aware he was being observed, so he tried to sit up as straight as possible without looking like he was trying too hard. He was gratified when the bartender walked away without calling an ambulance.

The next bar was less than a block away, but across the street. Not wanting to waste time, Aria had been crisscrossing back and forth through traffic in order to hit every bar along the way. Business had picked up again and at times she found herself in line, waiting for her chance to transmit the requisite information.

In one of those lines at a Mexican place called Bakersfield, she inadvertently got trapped behind and between a particularly healthy-looking group of women hovering in tight formation right by the bar. Rendered immobile, Aria's predicament was compounded by her own slight physique, a disability that prevented her from muscling her way to the bartender.

Once Aria determined that the ladies preventing her from reaching her destination were showing no sign of moving or were even aware of Aria's presence, she took decisive action. First, she shoved her hand through a hole that miraculously appeared between two of the ladies' bodies and grabbed the edge of the bar. Once sure of her grip, she then used her handhold as an anchor with which to pull herself through the convention of flesh obstructing her from her target.

Having achieved her objective, the heavy-set trio of women against whom she had been waging a quiet battle for space no longer seemed interested in occupying the territory and distributed themselves more evenly into the void between the bar and the dining tables, allowing Aria to relax and patiently wait her turn.

Standing there, it occurred to Aria she was hungry, that she had not eaten anything since before her shift at Liberty's. She decided to kill two birds with one stone so, after reciting her spiel about her search for Jack to the bartender, she ordered some chips and salsa, a couple tacos, and a beer. By the time they arrived, Aria was ravenous, and quite nearly inhaled the freshly made corn chips. Indeed, it wasn't until her tongue started to burn from the salsa that she decided to slow her intake. That was also the moment she was reminded she was alone. Had she been with anyone, simply anyone, they both could have laughed at the ridiculousness of her burning tongue, but she knew that kind of thing is only interesting in the moment, and only to people who cared enough to be sharing that moment with you in the first place.

From her perch at the bar, though surrounded by humanity, there was no one who would find it amusing that she had been overcome by spices. And, if she attempted to share her tale with any of the strangers sitting or standing close by, she would surely come off as weird or crazy.

Knowing all that, she did the logical thing.

She kept it to herself.

There was a moment, a fuzzy moment, after Aria paid the bill but before she was out the door, that she saw someone she recognized, or at least thought she recognized. Not Bill, however. No. Two times in one night would have been too much. This was someone else. She was not far from the door and saw him walking past the windows, but her view was obstructed by the crowd in the bar and the crowd on the street and she didn't really get a good look. For a moment, she believed the person to be her first boyfriend, Brian. But by the time she made it to the street Brian, or Would-Be-Brian had disappeared, leading her to believe she really hadn't seen him at all, that she had seen a ghost.

What is in that salsa?

It wasn't the first time this sort of thing had happened. Over the last five or six years, she had experienced a number of Brian sightings, some real and some imagined. After a few years of them, she began attributing the sightings to "Brian Regret," which was Aria's shorthand for the guilt she felt about how things had ended with her first love.

She met Brian in French class. At first, she found him a little hyperactive, though over time his energy grew on her. She was also put off by his choice of a name for French class. He chose Guy, which in Europe is

pronounced Gee. She had no idea why he would choose such a ridiculous sounding name or why it bothered her so much. She had chosen
"Chloe" for herself, a name she came to prefer to her own. But Bri-
an/Guy/Gee sat right next to her, and as much as she tried to ignore him,
she found it impossible to do so, mostly because he sat right next to her,
but also because he could be amusing. She would later learn that his
choice of Guy was an inside joke, with him as the only insider. He
thought it sounded funny, and Brian loved a good joke.

Their high school courtship coincided with the decline in Steffie's
mental health, and the family turmoil ushered in by her sister's descent
drove Aria ever closer to Brian, who could make her laugh and keep her
in the moment, and whose family members spoke to each other in calm,
relaxed voices.

This made a big difference for her. Since Aria was still a teenager,
she felt *everything*. Everything was new. Everything was important. She
was digesting so much of the world so quickly that she could barely
make any sense of it, but with Brian she didn't need to make sense of
anything. He was her calm in the storm. They were smitten, and after
only a few dates she was surprised by how much she needed him. Her
sanity resided in his sense of humor and the wet goat smell he exuded
about half the time. It turned out Brian/Guy/Gee was exactly what she
needed, and she was as surprised as anyone.

Aria held steady in front of Bakersfield, looking in the direction she
thought she saw him walking, not at all sure it was him, believing it
surely wasn't, but looking anyway. She couldn't stop herself. She did
not find him.

What happened a year later, in her first year of college, was her fault.
She slept with someone else, some other freshman boy with whom she
had a lighthearted, we're-both-new-to-this flirtation. She slept with him

at a party two weeks after Steffie killed herself and she got drunk and Brian wasn't there and she needed *not* to be alone.

She immediately felt guilty and convinced herself the best course of action was to keep it to herself, that it wasn't going to happen again and that she still loved Brian. The other boy had been a band-aid at best, she told herself. But there were no secrets in their circle of friends, and by Monday morning she was dealing with the fallout. Aria's teary-eyed confession of regret could not overcome Brian's teary-eyed admission of pain, and it was over. Just like that. They had not spoken since. The Brian sightings started soon after.

Aria reminded herself her current search, as far as she knew, had nothing to do with Brian, and moved on to the next bar.

Chapter Eleven

Friends and other Annoyances

Once the door was removed and the seat belts cut through, Jesse was able to lift the boy and blanket off Jack in one smooth motion. Jack immediately noticed a change in weight and gravity, as if nothing was holding him in place. Troy was no longer pressed against him. Then the light. What had been complete darkness under the protective blanket had been replaced with blinding, crinkled sunlight, flowing in through the honeycomb of crackled windshield. When Jack realized what was happening, he tried to move, tried to climb out of the ruin. Jesse's voice stopped him. "Don't move, Jack. You're hurt. We'll get you out in a second. Just don't move." Jack did as he was told.

8:27
I feel safe here.
I always have.
I mean, I know it's just a bar . . .

Jack had decided where he would go next. Now certifiably drunk and having completely abandoned his bar-hopping scheme, he made the command decision. Whilst still in Japp's, he somehow managed to roust himself from the couch on which he had been deposited, grab his coat and get outside. He was going to walk two blocks north on Main Street to MOTR, a bar he knew well. MOTR was an acronym, and Jack knew what the acronym stood for, but only because he had asked one of the bartenders late one Friday night, four or five years earlier.

"Hey, so why did they spell the name wrong?"

He had been searching the walls, looking for pictures of muscle cars and finding only band posters. The female bartender reacted to the query with a glare and in her best parent-talking-to-a-child voice, responded to the question she had long grown tired of answering.

"Music in Over the Rhine."

She might have finished the sentence with "you idiot," but Jack couldn't recall.

Besides not knowing what the acronym actually stood for, it had taken Jack a while to get the gist of the place. The rules at MOTR, he discovered, were simple. Live music was available every night, and no singer or band was ever allowed to play cover songs. It all had to be original, even on open-mic Tuesdays. Once fully cognizant of this zeitgeist, and after doing some math in his head, Jack was astounded at the prospect of having to book some six hundred or so bands every year. He was equally astounded by the revelation that 600 original-music bands existed within driving distance of Cincinnati. But there they were, night after night. Bands from Austin, Brooklyn, and points who knows where, along with plenty of local talent as well. Sometimes the bands were exceptional, sometimes less so, but they were always playing their own stuff, for good or ill.

8:27
Nothing bad can happen to me here.
Nothing bad has ever happened to me here.
Nothing bad will happen to me now.

Jack claimed the small table situated off the end of the bar. From this position, adjacent to the middle window, he could watch the snow and the people walking in it. He was happy. The table was isolated, in a way, despite its proximity to the bar.

The opening band was setting up when he arrived, testing instruments and wiring amplifiers on the stage at the opposite end of the barroom, the activity sufficient to keep the patrons' attention on the stage and away from Jack and the Drunk Log. For him, it was potentially the perfect situation, a busy bar offering anonymity in a crowd. Most likely, the only person who would approach him without an invitation was Jim, the trusty bartender, whom Jack knew from numerous previous encounters, and who possessed sufficient bartender-empathy to know when a guest wanted to engage in friendly conversation or be left alone.

Jack got a drink and focused on the log, which Jim did not acknowledge. He had seen plenty of that type of behavior in the bar before—writers and musicians with notebooks and artists with sketch pads. Though he didn't engage in such behavior himself, it didn't bother Jim that others did, as long as they didn't bother anyone or mind if the bar was a little sticky. He and the other bartenders understood MOTR was a magnet for music lovers and anti-social notebook-writers.

8:29
I just heard somebody order a High Life, and I mean they actually used the words "High Life."
Score one for the Miller Beer marketing department.
Who knew some well-placed advertising could persuade an entire generation
to call Miller Beer High Life?
In a world full of craft beer, the main attraction has to be the price, right?
I guess, honestly, who gives a crap. I'm sitting here with a four dollar draft myself.

Gotta love this place.

Okay—where was I?

That's right. Troy.

I remember the last time I saw him.

The concussion didn't erase my memory of it, even though I wished it had.

Here's a weird thing—there was no blood, at least not that I could see.

After Troy was out of the car, I remember thinking how weird it was that there was no blood.

Not from him and not from me.

Wait—that's not true.

We both had cuts, bloody cuts, but nothing crazy. Nothing like you'd see in a movie.

The lack of it made me think he might still be alive.

Stupid, fucking, hope. But nearly all of our damage was internal.

I thought that was unfair, that there was no blood.

I remember thinking there should be blood everywhere.

It would have made more sense.

It would have seemed more justified.

It would have made more sense.

Still, there's a stain, isn't there? Even if it's not a blood stain, it's still there.

A stain I can't wash out. The stain is on me, isn't it?

The stain is in me. IN me. It's in me the way he was in me.

It's okay.

It's just another stain added to all the unwashed stains that came before it.

Added to all the stupid shit I did and said before that day.

Added to everything I ever regret doing, all the mistakes.
What I've come to realize, Posterity, in case you haven't been
paying attention,
is that there is only one way to clean all this up.
All of the stains, all of the regrets, that were there before that
day . . .
Well, I suppose I could have lived with those.
But, after Troy, something had to give.

"Hey, Jack. What are you writing?"

What the fuck?

Aria finished her food and decided the man she had seen walking on the street hadn't been Brian. It couldn't be Brian. How could it have possibly been Brian? So instead of chasing after what she now believed to be a ghost, she turned north and continued the serpentine pattern she was so proud of inventing.

Aria managed her way in and out of several more bars before it occurred to her, again, that she might be wasting her time. It wasn't the same as earlier, when she worried she was wasting her time looking for Jack with no chance of helping him. This time, it was the idea that she might be slogging through the snow on her search while, quite possibly, he might be home, under a blanket, in front of the fireplace, watching television.

The serene scene she imagined only made her angry for a moment. She did not really believe he was home. The Voice was not telling her so. No, she believed he, too, was out slogging in the snow, going bar to bar, just like she was, and that eventually she would catch up to him.

To be on the safe side, however, Aria decided it couldn't hurt to double check. After all, she was only a couple blocks from the building that housed her employer as well as Jack's condo, so why not stop by, just in case? Another block or two would put her nearly parallel with Liberty's. From there it would be easy to hop over and knock on his door.

By the time Aria hit the sixth or seventh bar on Vine Street, she had the *Looking for Jack* script memorized. With each interaction, her proficiency increased, both at passing along the requisite information and garnering any news that might be helpful. Of the latter there had, as yet, been no revelations. Still, Aria began to enjoy this mushrooming efficiency, and not just because she felt it was helping her catch up to Jack.

She had begun to have a sense that something was stalking her, something she couldn't name, but that somehow, by moving faster, whatever thing might be following her would have a more difficult time doing so. Or so she believed. Though she couldn't put a name to the stalker, she had an inkling, as she had earlier, that it had something to do with Steffi.

If that were true, she thought, then allowing it to catch her would result in failing to stop Jack from meeting the same end as her sister, and that she could not bear. Aria, whatever was stalking her was also stalking Jack, but it was driving them to different ends. She hoped differently. She hoped her instinct was wrong, but it rarely had been in the past.

"Excuse me, Miss, can you help me get something to eat?"

The question from the shabbily dressed, middle-aged woman startled Aria. The old-lady panhandler seemed to appear out of thin air.

"I'm sorry, ma'am, I don't have any cash."

It was not a lie. Aria often carried cash, mostly tips earned during a shift behind the bar and had occasionally been known to hand some of it over to panhandlers. On this night, however, she left the bar before she had a chance to close out.

"I just want a sandwich. Can you buy me a sandwich?"

The panhandler was persistent and had apparently heard the I-don't-have-any cash excuse before. Even she, the panhandler, knew the world was moving toward a cashless society, but she also knew the sandwich shop took credit cards.

Aria was starting to get annoyed. She *was* on a mission, after all. But she stopped, took a breath, and decided to buy a sandwich for the chatty mendicant, who seemed genuinely grateful for the meal.

Though the sandwich-buying escapade took less than ten minutes to conclude, Aria was now anxious. She felt the need to get moving, to continue her undulating search pattern back and forth across Vine until finally reaching Kaze, a Japanese restaurant with a semi-detached bar.

Aria wasn't sure what the actual name of the semi-detached bar might be.

It might have had the same name as the restaurant, Kaze with the word "Bar" added, but she had never asked. The only indication that the bar existed at all was a neon sign, hanging about 10 feet over the sidewalk, with the word BAR blazing into the darkness. The sign itself was elegant in its simplicity. Non-descript, yet to the point. Clearly, the restaurant's management had not put a lot of thought into the name of the bar, and as a result, everyone Aria knew just referred to it as "that bar behind Kaze," or some version thereof. Despite the lack of specificity, the description was more than the locals needed and enough for the uninitiated to find their way.

Aria stomped the snow off her boots as she entered, garnered the bartender's attention, and ran through her *Finding Jack* script, complete with pictures. This was her jumping off point. From here, she would go and check if Jack had found his way home. It was just three blocks.

Kevin was a regular at MOTR, at least on Open Mic Night, just as Jack had been, though Jack's reason to be there on Tuesdays was different than Kevin's. Kevin came to perform, to hone his craft, so to speak, and build an audience.

Jack showed up on Tuesdays to eat dinner and check out the local talent, some of which was horrible and some quite good. Most of what happened on Open Mic Night, while not awful, was less than memorable, and Kevin's performances tended to fall into that category. But he was friendly, earnest about his hobby, and brave enough to stand up in front of strangers on a weekly basis and play a couple of his songs for them.

This was something Jack could never have seen himself doing, so he respected Kevin for putting himself out like that, especially as he had never found the courage to do it himself. Granted, to date he had yet to display a talent worthy of an audience. He was not a musician, a comedian, nor a poet, which were the three most common schticks on Tuesday nights.

Jack had flirted with the idea of writing a poem and reading it on stage, not because he particularly liked poetry but because it seemed like the easiest of the three routines. After watching other poets read their material, Jack was of the mind that he could write something resembling a poem, so long as the words were of a certain meter and form. The topic didn't seem to matter at all. He could write a poem about a stray cat and for his efforts receive polite applause, at least, and maybe a few chuckles if the cat was funny. Outside of music, poetry, or comedy there was, occasionally, a burlesque stripper. Jack did not find her performance particularly enjoyable. Physically, she was not what Jack looked for in the opposite sex, but he afforded to her the same baseline of credit he afforded all the Tuesday night acts: They were brave to do their thing, whatever that thing may be, in front of a bunch of strangers.

"What are you writing?" Kevin asked again.

"Oh, nothing really, Kevin."

Jack snapped the notebook shut and slid the pen into the spiral binding without looking down, no small achievement given his rising alcohol level. He held Kevin's attention, figuring if Kevin was looking at him, he wasn't looking at the log.

"That's cool."

Kevin, being a notebook scribbler himself, really was interested in what Jack might be doing. He had actually encouraged Jack's poetry scheme in the past, though clearly to no avail.

"Mayhap I buy you a beer?"

"Mayhap?"

"Just a word I'm trying out. Lemme buy you a beer. I owe you."

Mayhap?

Kevin owed Jack a number of beers. One of Jack's methods of support for the Open Mic acts was to buy performers drinks, especially ones he liked. Though Kevin wasn't a very good singer, he was a decent guitarist and, as well, displayed the aforementioned earnestness that Jack appreciated in unpaid performers.

It wasn't that Kevin, or anyone else, couldn't afford to buy their own drinks. Most of them had day jobs, or reasonable facsimiles, providing them sufficient wherewithal to buy drinks for themselves on a weeknight, but Jack liked to do it anyway. For reasons he didn't spend any time examining, the purchasing of drinks for near-strangers made him feel like part of the ad-hoc group that formed in MOTR every Tuesday night. It was Jack's way of being part of something in which he otherwise found himself unable to participate.

"Can I buy you a beer?"

Kevin asked again, forcing Jack to give him his attention.

"Oh, sure. Thanks, Kevin." *Wait, what?*

Jack surprised himself by saying yes. He had a nearly-full beer sitting right in front of him. He was also surprised by the fact he didn't immediately shoo Kevin away, treating him as a nuisance.

Maybe I'm in the mood for some company, he thought. Although if he actually did want some company, he wasn't sure why. Until that moment, Jack had been perfectly happy to spend the night alone, writing his memoir in solitary anonymity. But there he was, welcoming Kevin's interruption, and when Kevin turned to order drinks at the bar, he made sure to take a few gulps of the beer he had purchased for himself., the full one sitting in front of him. It would be rude to maintain a full glass of beer while waiting for another, and by the time Kevin turned around, hands full of newly purchased beers, Jack managed to finish off more than half of his original.

"So, . . . are you going to tell me what you're writing?"

Kevin sat down across from Jack as he asked the question.

"Oh, you know, just my thoughts."

Jack demurred, but gave Kevin some truth. He wanted to change the topic.

"So . . . Kevin, what have you been writing?"

Kevin reached into his back pocket and pulled out his own notebook, well-worn and, by the look of it, probably nearly full of Kevin's words. He took a slug of his beer and motioned for Jack to do the same.

"You show me yours and I'll show you mine."

He smiled at Jack and took a drink.

"Seriously."

Fuck.

Jack, despite his receding sobriety, felt vaguely panicked by Kevin's insistence, and did his best to be forthright with the man who just bought him a drink.

"Honestly, Kevin, I'm not ready to show this to anybody. You get that, right?"

"Hell yes, I do."

Kevin responded without hesitation. Opening his shabby notebook, he held it over the table, riffled the pages like he was trying to make sure none of them were sticking together. "Most of the stuff in here is crap, Jack. Most of it is not worth reading, not even by me. Definitely not by anyone else."

Kevin laughed, took another swig and set his beer on top of the tattered cover of his notebook.

"It makes a good coaster, though."

Jack had never seen Kevin like this. Usually, he found him to be something of an introvert, but that night he was downright brash.

"Are you drunk?"

Kevin spent a moment pondering the question.

"Absolutely. I'm a little high, too. Why do you ask?"

"I don't know . . . you seem different. Maybe it's because I've never seen you high before?"

"I don't get high on Tuesday's, Jack. It's a school night. Tonight's Friday and I don't work tomorrow. I can do whatever I want. I can drink all night. I can write all night. I can even try to get laid. I'll bet at least two of those things will happen."

Kevin laughed at himself again. Jack tried to smile but he wasn't sure what the muscles in his face were actually doing.

"What about you? Are you drunk? High? Both?"

Jack took a deep breath.

"Just drunk."

Jack felt sure there was now a smile forming on his face. Kevin's verve was infectious. "But I plan to get drunker."

Kevin smacked the table with his right hand.

"Cheers to that, brother. Maybe you'll get drunk enough to tell me what you're hiding in that book."

"I doubt it, Kevin, but you never know."

But Jack *did* know. He wasn't going to show Kevin anything, and despite the fact he was enjoying Kevin's company, he knew if he was going to be able to continue with the Drunk Log, he would have to find a way to distract him and send him on his merry way. He began plotting while Kevin started in on a dissertation about his poor singing skills, lack of luck with women, and selected other personal tragedies.

Chapter Twelve

One More at MOTR

They were moving Jack. It was the first time since he was a child he could remember being carried. Jesse placed a gurney next to the opening where the driver's door used to be, and now he and another fireman were lifting Jack from the car, placing him on the clean white sheet of the gurney. Jack couldn't see the sheet. He just assumed it was white. He had stopped crying and was now making assumptions about the color of the sheet on the gurney, swooning just as they covered his mouth and nose with the oxygen mask. What were they asking him? Something about his leg? He tried to answer but he wasn't sure if words were able to penetrate the silicone of the mask.

"Well, I gotta hit the head."

Kevin stood, making a show of adjusting his pants.

"Don't wait up, Dad. It might be a while."

To the best of Jack's knowledge, Kevin had never served in the Navy, so he wasn't sure why he substituted "head" for "bathroom." Of course, Jack really had very little background on Kevin. The extent of his personal knowledge was that Kevin worked at a local software firm and had moved to Cincinnati from some other part of the Midwest. He did not know what Kevin actually did at the software firm, or from what city he had moved. It was too late to ask now.

"Take your time."

I'm at MOTR. Still.

Kevin's bugging me but he's in the bathroom so I'm going to write for a few minutes.

Other than Kevin, the people in the bar seem to grasp the isolation of this table here by the window. It might as well have a force field around it.

Because of Kevin, I'm now on my ninth or tenth drink, I think.

Let me think.

Jack thought for a moment, going through each drink he thought he had consumed thus far, one by one. He kept losing count, though, and had to start over, so he grabbed his notebook and started to write.

8:50

Yup. I'm ninety percent sure this is number ten.

Maybe number eleven?

Either way, I gotta say, I'm drunk but not as drunk as I thought I'd be by now.

Not sure how I'm still walking. I'm going to slow it down, though.

I should drink some water.

The band just did a sound check. They'll probably start playing soon.

Wait, Ten or eleven?

Not sure what type of music they're going to play, but they sounded good just now.

Folky-rock?

Doesn't matter.

I'm sure it will be fine. Did I mention that I'm feeling pretty drunk?

Here's the thing . . . wait.

What was I going to talk about?

The band just started playing. They sound good so far.

No idea what happened to Kevin. Seems like he's been gone for a long time.

Here's the thing, I'm blown away by people who can write a good song.

I mean, you pack all kinds of shit into that three or four minutes.

I think a good songwriter could take all the words I've written in this damn notebook

and gel it down to a four-minute song.

I actually fear that could be done, because that might mean that all these words aren't worth the effort.

Wait.

It just occurred to me that I'm worried if all this would be a good song or not.

I mean, what if all of this isn't even worthy of a song? Not even three minutes of usable crap?

Wait.

Is that where that saying came from?

Something isn't worth a song? Okay, I'm rambling.

Bottom line is - I'm jealous of good songwriters.

I've tried it.

I tried writing a song for a girlfriend in college.

It was awful.

Okay. I remember why I started on all this.

Troy loved the Beatles.

Mostly, he loved the song Hard Day's Night.

Even though the song isn't that complicated, I'm pretty sure Troy didn't really get it.

How could he? He was only seven.

But, man, he loved that song.

He made me play it whenever we got in my car and then we'd
sing it together.

He could listen to it ten times in a row.

Without having been asked, Kevin appeared with two glasses of water. Jack did not initially take notice of his return, either because his movements were silent or because the background noise in the bar covered any sound that might have announced his arrival. When he finally did notice, Jack wasn't sure how long Kevin had been standing there, potentially reading the log. It didn't really matter to Jack anymore, however. Either he was too drunk to care or believed that, most likely, Kevin was unable to read sloppy, upside-down handwriting.

"You're like a ninja."

"Well, not technically, Jack. I mean, I'm not certified or anything like that. But I am pretty quiet." Kevin set two glasses of water down on the table before sitting across from Jack.

"Certified? You are really a man of many colors, Kevin."

"I did pretty well on the final exam, but I never officially graduated. You know. Politics."

Jack nodded and laughed, wondering for an instant if he should continue the joke. He decided against it. He had yet to determine how long he was actually willing to sit there with Kevin, let alone deplete his waning mental acuity to keep a joke about ninjas moving forward.

Jack's drinking had slowed, and though he finished his first MOTR beer, the one Kevin bought for him earlier remained full to the brim, sitting quietly on the table in front of him. He had forgotten to ask Kevin for water and was pleased he thought of it on his own. He was also hoping Kevin washed his hands after completing his bathroom business.

Jack understood that in a couple hours Kevin's toilet habits would be of no concern, but that fact didn't abridge his own desire to avoid the unintentional ingestion of his temporary table-mate's bodily fluids.

"Thanks for the water, Kevin."

Jack forced himself not to mention hand washing despite the fact that Kevin's potentially unsterile fingers had positioned themselves pretty high on the glass, near the top, where one puts one's lips. He decided to take his chances.

Livin' on the edge, before I go over it . . .

"Cheers."

Reaching the northern terminus of the bar scene on Vine, Aria took a moment to rest before making the short hike to Jack's. The snow had picked up its pace and she needed a drink and to let her coat dry, at least for a few minutes. Her sense of urgency hadn't disappeared, but she understood her course of action to be as logical as it could be, given the expanse of possibilities when it came to finding Jack. Besides, people in the neighborhood were always randomly running into one another. That being the case, part of Aria was hoping for that sort of lucky encounter, as long as it wasn't a former boyfriend. It was great to have a plan, but it couldn't hurt to hope for a little magic.

"Can I get a Sapporo?"

When the bartender brought her beer, she ran the script and settled onto a bar chair, hanging her wet coat on a hook under the bar overhang.

Aria gave the place a once-over, looking around to see if she knew anyone who might also know Jack, but didn't immediately recognize anyone with these requisite qualities. There were plenty of familiar faces, people she had seen around, but no one she could be sure about, no one she was willing to randomly question on the whereabouts of her . . . what?

Friend? Acquaintance? Salvation project? Potential boy . . .?

She struggled for a moment to classify her relationship with Jack. In the end, she settled on "sort-of-boyfriend," knowing the description was woefully inadequate. Sort-of-boyfriend couldn't begin to describe the complexity of what was going on at the moment. For that, she was going to have to keep thinking. She made a mental note to sit Jack down and discuss their relationship at the earliest possible convenience. He owed her that much.

Sipping her beer in supposed obscurity, Aria allowed her thoughts to drift away from the hunt for Jack. They didn't wander anywhere particularly important. In fact, once released from any thoughts regarding her search, Aria's mind turned easily to the more mundane aspects of her day-to-day existence. Her work schedule over the next couple of weeks, how much longer she could go without cleaning her apartment, and the pile of clothes mushrooming out of the hamper all received some consideration.

Sufficiently lost in these routine thoughts, Aria at first didn't recognize her best friend from high school had taken the bar stool next to her. Tracy stared at her for a good fifteen seconds before Aria turned to look at her. Even then it took a moment to register.

"Tracy? What the hell?"

Aria stood to embrace her old friend, receiving the same in return.

"I haven't seen you in months. I wish I had known you were coming down here tonight!"

"I'm supposed to meet my mother here for dinner, but she's running late, as usual, so I figured I'd come back here for a drink. If I thought I would have had time to see you, I would have let you know."

The two old friends followed along with each other's lives as best they could on social media, occasionally making comments on the other's posts, but social media is no substitute for real human contact, so the joy each felt to run into the other was palpable.

"Let me buy you a drink."

Aria, in the process of sitting back down on her highchair, was knocked toward the bar, and into her beer, by someone trying to shove their way into the small space between Aria and Tracy. Tracy started laughing and Aria laughed with her, though she felt sorry for the bartender, who was already cleaning up the spill as Aria, out of habit, worked furiously to absorb the stray beer the with bar napkins.

"Aria, you must be the least coordinated dancer I've ever known, at least off the dance floor."

They hugged again.

As children, they had spent years in dance classes together.

"Now, why don't you let me buy you another drink?"

"That would be wonderful."

Aria allowed the bartender to finish cleaning up her mess and managed to get back onto her barstool without further incident.

"How's your mom doing?"

"She's doing okay, I think. We're running up on the one-year anniversary of Dad's death, so we're taking turns getting her out of the house. Tonight was supposed to be Teddy's turn but his youngest is sick so we traded nights."

Tracy fell into a discussion of her family as if no time had passed since last seeing Aria in person, which happened to be at her father's funeral. Aria was acutely aware of this fact, and felt her face flush while Tracy brought her up to date, embarrassed by her current lack of intimate involvement in the life of her friend.

"Are you okay?"

Tracy looked as if she was examining Aria's face for skin cancer.

"I'm good. How come?"

"Well, you just look, I don't know, a little anxious? Maybe a little preoccupied? I feel like I may have interrupted something when I sat down. What's on your mind?"

Aria decided to come clean, but not about Jack. She didn't want her old friend to think she was nuts.

"Well, right now I'm feeling guilty about not being there for you like I should be. I feel like I've been so selfish lately. I haven't even offered to watch Leila . . ."

Tracy cut Aria off with a wave of her hand.

"Stop it. You've had plenty of your own life to deal with. Besides, it's not like I've been calling you every day, asking you to come over. Trust me, a two-year-old is not as much fun as you might think. They scream a lot and they climb on everything."

"I'm still sorry, Tracy. I should be a better friend."

Tracy wiped a tear from Aria's eye.

"I will say this, though, I'm kicking your ass on the whole marriage and family thing." She smiled at Aria, her expression explaining that none of that really mattered. "C'mon, we're here together now, at least until Mom shows up. Let's reminisce. Remember that time you were making out with Teddy and Dad caught you?"

Aria certainly remembered making out with her best friend's brother. The embarrassment of being discovered in the act by Tracy's father eliminated any chance it would ever happen again. Her father, full of caustic wit, quipped without hesitation:

"Should you need one, I have extra condoms."

That, as they say, was that.

Kevin showed no sign of retreating to some other corner of the bar. Indeed, to Jack it appeared Kevin's ass had grown roots into the bar stool on which he was perched. Jack marveled at the way Kevin was able to blithely dismiss, or perhaps even consider, that he was an uninvited guest. Unbeknownst to Jack, however, the impetus for Kevin's seemingly dogged determination to remain at the two-top with Jack was one of simple fear. Kevin hated being alone in bars and restaurants or in any place where common custom dictated the presence of another human being, of "company."

On that evening, Kevin's yearning for live music was sufficient motivation to get him out of his apartment and into MOTR. But temporarily overcoming his often-stultifying social anxiety did not prevent him from glomming onto the first not-alone opportunity to present itself. That opportunity presented itself in the form of Jack.

Though Jack always seemed like a nice guy, until then Kevin hadn't developed a particular affection or affinity for his company. Jack just happened to be the first person he recognized when he entered the bar. Jack had the added benefit of being alone, a combination Kevin found irresistible. Indeed, he found it irresistible enough to be willing to buy Jack beer for as long as he was willing to stay seated at the table with him. Of all this, Jack was blissfully ignorant, though most likely the knowledge of Kevin's strategy wouldn't have changed the situation.

Jack, at least at the moment, found Kevin to be a not-too-unpleasant combination of distraction and annoyance. During the time it took the band to finish its warm-up and play the first three songs from its set list, he had allowed Kevin to blather on about his ex-girlfriend (Penny), the hot dogs he ate for dinner (burnt), and his apartment's state of cleanliness (three on a scale of 10, 10 being the cleanest.)

The amount of attention Jack was able to pay to any individual part of Kevin's free-range ramblings was largely dependent on how much he liked whatever song was being played at the time. Naturally, the better the song the less attention paid. But despite his attempts to focus solely on particularly good songs, Kevin's voice demonstrated an ability to needle its way into his aural cavities. Jack needed to break the cycle.

"Kevin."

The sharpness of Jack's voice caught Kevin by surprise.

"What is it, Jack?"

"Kevin, do you know what *Terminal Velocity* means?"

"Hmmm . . . Isn't that an action movie with Arnold Schwarzenegger?"

Jack stopped to think.

Could that be true? Was it an action movie with Arnold Schwarzenegger?

"Is it?"

"Yeah, I think so. No, wait, I think it's actually with Charlie Sheen. Yeah. It's kinda old. Like from the 90's."

"Charlie Sheen was in an action movie called *Terminal Velocity*?"

Now Jack was confused.

"Yup. I think so. I think he was also in *Apocalypse Now*. Or was it his brother, Emilio Estevez? I can never remember which one was in what movie."

"What? Wait. Charlie Sheen wasn't in *Apocalypse Now*. I think it was his dad, Martin Sheen, who was in that one. It definitely wasn't Emilio Estevez. He was in all those Brat Pack movies."

Jack stopped to think. "Yup. I'm sure it was Martin Sheen."

"Are you sure? I swear I thought Charlie Sheen was in *Apocalypse*."

"No way. Had to be his dad."

"Emilio?"

"No, dumbass, his dad Martin. Emilio is his brother."

"Wait, Emilio is Charlie's brother? Their names are so different. How does that work?"

Things had gotten off track. Jack did not pose the question to get a movie history lesson on the Sheen/Estevez family or dive into the various and sundry character portrayals of any of its members. By then, he wasn't sure if any of them had been in any movie.

"It was *Apocalypse Now*, right? Now just *Apocalypse*."

"No, Kevin. Stop for a second. I was asking if you knew what *Terminal Velocity* means."

"Oh, got it."

Kevin took a sip of beer, thought for a second and answered decisively.

"Nope."

"Okay. Listen up, Kevin. Terminal Velocity is the maximum speed a body can fall, depending on its posture and the air pressure. It takes something like ten to fourteen seconds to get that speed, which is around 120 miles an hour."

Kevin seemed to be thinking.

"Got it, Jack. Now, do you wanna tell me why I need to know that?"

Jack squinted.

"What? Are you an engineer or something?"

"Yes, I am an engineer, Kevin. You didn't know that?"

"Nope. I don't think you've ever mentioned it before."

Kevin lost interest in the conversation. Unlike Jack, he would have preferred a discussion of the Sheen family's film credits. Any hope Jack had of engaging Kevin in a discussion of suicidal falling speeds melted into one of the band's songs.

Jack wouldn't bring it up again.

"Mom just cancelled."

Tracy had been checking her phone every couple of minutes for just such a message.

"I figured she would, with the snow and all. Looks like she's even late with cancellations."

Tracy was actually relieved. She was having a good time with her old friend.

"Figured."

"Well, looks like I have the evening free. You want to go get a drink somewhere else?" Tracy motioned for the check and packed her phone into her purse before Aria had a chance to answer. She was caught off guard. She had not expected to see Tracy at all, let alone receive an invitation to spend the night drinking with her.

Her first reaction was to say no, that she had other plans, but she feared a rejection would trigger an interrogation. She had neither the desire to tell Tracy what she was really up to, nor had she the time to develop an elaborate lie. On the fly, she decided to go with at least some of the truth and incorporate Tracy into her search.

"Sure. I was just going over to Liberty's anyway."

If Tracy wanted to go bar hopping with her old friend she couldn't have picked a better night.

"Perfect. Let's go."

Tracy stood, donned her down filled, stadium jacket.

"Ooh! Can we walk next door? I heard they tore down the old Kroger and I want to see the rubble."

Aria, initially surprised by the request to view the ruin of an old grocery store, found herself intrigued.

"That actually sounds kinda fun."

The demolished building was only a half block away, and though surrounded by fencing, they were able to get close enough to stare in awe at the piles of dirt, brick and related detritus of the former neighborhood grocery. The decades-old workhorse had been replaced by a shiny, new one some four blocks away, rendering the old one superfluous.

Aria, who did not live far from the ruin, felt an odd sense of empti-
ness. She had witnessed some of the demolition over the last few days,
but the snow-capped piles of rubble, resting in the now-dark expanse in
the middle of the city, somehow made her feel lonely. Tracy's voice
pried her from her meditation.

"Alright. I'm good. Just more piles of dirt."

Chapter Thirteen

Friends and Would-be Lovers

Jack knew he was in an ambulance but didn't remember how he got there. He could feel the oxygen mask on his face and could see two faces hovering over him. The eyes of the hovering faces seemed concerned. The eyes were not looking at his face. He could hear the siren and feel the bumps in the road. At one point, he felt a prick in his arm. He lazily assumed it must be an intravenous needle, most likely being used to pump in pain killers. He knew Troy was not with him.

9:29

Kevin just left the table. He's over there by the stage, in front of the speakers, at least for now.

Not sure how long he will be gone. I think all the engineering talk scared him away.

Plus, I think he's finally fuzzy or buzzy enough to stand by the stage all by himself.

I'll keep writing.

I'm drunker than Kevin, I think, but not drunk enough to erase memories.

I've tried that before, drinking to erase memories, I mean, and ended up in some pretty weird places, and not just physically. I mean, my mind likes to play tricks on me.

My drunk mind, I mean, likes to play tricks on me.

My drunk mind tries to convince me that I'm smarter than I am, that I'm stronger than I really am.

It will try to convince me that I'm super-attractive and that all the ladies love me,
and all kinds of other things that I really want to believe, but really don't.
And that's the good stuff.
I haven't even covered the bad stuff, mostly because the good stuff causes enough problems.
Believe it or not, I've discovered that very few women enjoy being hit on by a super-drunk guy. Surprised? So was I . . . apparently.
Luckily for me, I never did anything too stupid in front of Aria.
I was always careful about that.
For some reason I wanted to be better in front of her.
Can't have her thinking I'm an idiot, can I, Posterity?
Can't have her thinking I'm just another drunk guy at the bar, the same kind of guy she sees all the time.
Did I mention the bad stuff? Well, the bad stuff is pretty much the same as the good stuff,
mostly because the good stuff, the things your brain tries to convince you you're capable of
when you're hammered, can make you do ugly, stupid things.
It can make you do things you wince about in the shower the next morning.
It's all fun and games until somebody gets their feelings hurt.
Or tosses their cookies.
Still, the worst thing my brain tells me,
the worst thing it tries to convince me of when I'm wasted,
is that I really can forget.
I suppose that's the thing I really want,
which is why my brain tries to convince me I can have it.

What I really want, what I really need, I think,
is the forgiveness that comes with the forgetting.

Jack put the pen down and read the last entry, surprised by its clarity and dearth of mistakes, especially in light of his alcohol consumption so far. Counting again on his fingers, he guessed (again) that he was up to either ten or eleven drinks. He was confident the count was neither nine, nor twelve, and so must be one of the two numbers in between those two numbers.

Could I be drunker than I feel or feel less drunk than I am?

He began thinking that he should be at least a little drunker than he actually felt. Jack then began wondering if it was possible that he had somehow plateaued, that he had ultimately reached a level of drunkenness that could not be exceeded, no matter how much more he consumed.

The thought threw him into a bit of a panic. Was a plateau even possible? Could his own body's ability to process alcohol actually be saving him from himself? Or was this booze wall, perhaps, inevitable?

Jack could, after all, remember being much drunker on any number of occasions. He knew the way he felt now, with the room not even spinning, not even a little bit, that he had a long way to go in order to achieve maximum inebriation. He figured it would require a higher level of commitment, that if he was really serious about all the forgiving and forgetting, he would just have to put his nose to the grindstone.

9:39
I am drunk enough to say some things I don't want to forget.
Watch me now, Posterity.
Except for that last day, I don't want to forget anything about
my nephew.

I don't want to forget my family, generally speaking, either,
even though they may want me to.
Before that day we all got along pretty well.
I don't want to forget the dog I had when I was a kid. Mickey.
I could have done without the pillow-humping,
but nearly everything else about that dog was just fine.
I don't want to forget the first girl I kissed (Rebecca,)
or losing my virginity (Jennifer.)
I don't want to forget kissing Aria.
Certainly not that night.
Actually, I remember it like it was yesterday,
which shouldn't be a problem considering it wasn't that long
ago.
Not sure what it was then, what it was about her, I mean.
I mean, what it IS about her.
She's probably still on her shift at Liberty's.
I should probably stop by and see her once more.
Nope.
Bad idea.
I won't leave if I see her.
Okay—I'm way off track, I think.
How did I get to talking about Aria?
Ah! I was talking about the good things I want to remember.
Yup—I guess, looking at what I just wrote,
it looks like I want to remember nearly everything.
If that's the case, you might be asking yourself,
then why do I mean to kill myself?
Well, I've put a lot of thought into that, as you can imagine.
Here's my answer—all those good things don't equal the one,
unbelievably bad thing.

I tried, Posterity, I really did.

But it hasn't gotten any better and may have even gotten worse over the last year.

Early on I thought I could do it. Time heals all wounds, right?

But it hasn't really worked out that way.

The leg still hurts. It still burns.

The limp is still there.

Actually, that part is okay. Sort of a penance, I suppose. I could live with that.

It's the rest of it.

"What are you writing about?"

Kevin had again snuck up to the table, causing Jack's arm to jerk in surprise. The pen, loosed from the grip of Jack's fingers, went sailing past Kevin's ear, landing somewhere on the floor amongst the crowd of music fans.

"You want me to pick that up for you?"

"That would be great, if you can find it."

Jack didn't relish the opportunity to expend the time and effort involved in the acquisition of a new pen, but additionally had no desire to crawl around on the undoubtedly sticky, beer-befouled floor, looking for the instrument he had been carting around all night. He watched as Kevin weaved into the crowd, using his good manners and cell phone light to search for, and eventually find, Jack's pen.

Impressive.

"Here you go, buddy."

Jack examined the pen, which appeared to have suffered no damage on its round-trip journey from the table to the barroom floor and back.

"Thanks, Kevin."

"So . . . what are you writing about?"

Kevin's beer-induced persistence was becoming annoying. Jack searched his brain for the next distraction.

Due to weather-related issues, Aria and Tracy did not dawdle at the ruin of the old grocery store. It wasn't that the pile of rubble lacked in ability to fascinate, it was that the wind had started to pick up and the piles of dirt provided little protection from the blowing snow. Once they were back on 14th, however, and headed toward Liberty's, the surrounding buildings afforded them some cover from the evolving winter storm.

"You sure you want to do this? I think it's starting to get icy out here."

Aria was wearing hiking boots and therefore making her way with relative ease compared to her friend, whose knee-high boots were built more for fashion than for utility.

Tracy struggled to find footing.

"I'm good. They're slippery, but comfortable. No worries. I took a car service into the city, so it doesn't matter where I end up. Besides, if it gets too bad, I'll just stay at your place."

Something about the idea of Tracy staying overnight in her apartment did not sit well with Aria, though she couldn't quite figure out why. She shouldn't have a problem with her once-best-friend crashing on her couch during a winter storm.

Jeez, she thought, *it should actually be fun.*

So why did the thought of it make her uncomfortable? The answer came to her when they were closer to the orange building that housed both Liberty's Bar and Bottle and Jack's apartment. As they neared the rear of the tenement, she figured out why she didn't want Tracy to spend the night.

Jack.

What Aria figured out was that what she really wanted was for Jack to spend the night, and not on her couch. Or perhaps she would end up spending the night at his place. Either way, it didn't matter as long as one of them was spending the night at the other's place. There was no role for Tracy in either scenario.

"Sure. Let's see what happens."

Aria tried to sound upbeat. After all, no decision had to be made at the moment. Regardless, the chances of her friend crashing in her living room were slim. Tracy had children and a husband at home and, bearing that in mind, Aria figured she probably wouldn't have to be the villain, the selfish friend. At least not yet.

The snow-covered street delivering them to the front door of the bar was called Melindy, though Melindy was little more a wide alley than an actual street. To Aria, the benefit of taking Melindy was that it took her right past Jack's windows and door, but she was disappointed by the look of the place. The tall windows of the condominium were dark. They were dark in a way they shouldn't be on a normal Friday night. They were dark in a way that told her Jack wasn't there.

She kept moving with Tracy until they turned the corner and arrived at Liberty's. The bar, packed with bodies, felt warm and close after their trek through walk in the wind and snow. Aria, initially uneasy at the sight of Jack's darkened windows, felt a bit lighter by the warm ambience and interior of the bar.

"Can I get you a drink?"

Aria, preoccupied, had almost forgotten about Tracy, though she was standing right next to her.

"Yeah, Tracy, that would be great. Let me get them, though. I know people. What are you having?"

"A red wine would be great."

Aria smiled and waved to grab Aaron's attention. There was another tender behind the bar now, though she was new and Aria didn't know her that well.

"Hey! You're back! Are you working or drinking?"

Aaron smiled from across the bar.

"Drinking."

Aria smiled back.

"I'm done working tonight. I found somebody to take my shift."

"Good one. You're funny."

Aaron feigned annoyance.

"What can I get for you?"

"Can I get two reds? Maybe the Malbec?"

"You bet, but aren't you on a mission, or something like that?"

Aria demurred.

My mission, which I've already chosen to accept . . .

She didn't know how to explain her wild-goose-chase to her coworker, or to anyone, for that matter.

"Well, sort of. Ended up meeting up with my friend over there."

Aria pointed over her shoulder at Tracy.

"Sweet."

Aaron was already pouring the wine.

"Your friend's hot."

"Yeah, I suppose she is. She's also married, with children."

Aria gave a little laugh, punctuating Aaron's lack of luck. She was happy that Tracy's presence was enough to interrupt Aaron's line of questioning.

"Too bad."

Aaron handed her the glasses of wine and declined her attempt to pay.

"You know better than that."

Aria smiled and turned to hand a glass of wine to Tracy, who had procured some space at one of the stand-up islands in the center of the bar. The island had been fully occupied when the two first entered, but Tracy was good at making room where there appeared to be none.

"Nice job."

Aria was pleased to be reminded of her friend's particular social skills.

"My pleasure."

Tracy took a sip of the Malbec and leaned across the island until she could almost whisper in Aria's ear.

"Do you want to tell me what's going on with you?"

Aria was taken by surprise and hoped her expression did not reflect it. Tracy pulled back to the other side of the island and was now staring at her, clearly waiting for some sort of answer. She could hardly tell her best friend that, for reasons not yet fully understood, she was chasing one of her customers from bar to bar, a customer with whom she shared a kiss, exactly once, who she was now trying to make sure didn't go off somewhere and kill himself.

But it was a really good kiss . . .

Tracy, of course, was well aware of the circumstances of Steffi's demise and the toll it had taken on Aria's family and would, quite naturally, assume her childhood friend had gone off the deep end. Simultaneously, Aria feared any story she might try to make up on the spot would, in short order, have numerous holes punched into it by her astute friend. She needed to think quickly, however, because Tracy had not averted her eyes, or even blinked. The clock was ticking.

"Well, this is going to sound a little crazy."

Aria figured she could preface her soon-to-be-told lie with a bit of truth, a dab of which always helped to make a lie sound a little less like a lie.

"Try me."

"Okay, shit. One of the guys, one of the regulars here at the bar, well, he and I sort of agreed to meet this evening for a drink. I think I must have missed him, though."

Aria was delighted at how truthful her lie seemed, even to her.

Tracy stared at Aria with widening eyes, waiting for more details.

"You were supposed to meet him at Kaze? Is that why I saw you in there tonight?"

Aria, astounded that Tracy was actually helping to flesh out the lie for her, barely hid her joy.

"Uh, yup. That's exactly what happened. Then I figured, you know, after missing him at Kaze, that he might have tried showing up over here, since this is where I work, and all. Makes sense, right?"

"Absolutely. But don't you have his phone number? Can't you just call him to see what's going on?"

Aria felt her face flush, mostly with anger at modern technology, but also because she now had to come up either with a plausible excuse for not having Jack's telephone number, which she did, indeed, have, or explain why the number didn't work. She decided to run with the latter.

"Um, yeah, well, I tried it and got no answer. I suppose he could have dropped it or not heard it or something like that. That happens, right?"

"Oh, of course, but doesn't he have your number? Wouldn't he try to call you?"

"Well, damn Tracy, I guess so, but if he dropped it or left it at home . . ."

Aria's voice went up about half an octave. Tracy's persistence was getting under her skin. Couldn't she just keep helping Aria construct the lie?

"Maybe you should try him again."

"Can we drop this, please?"

"Well, damn Kevin. You're getting kind of relentless about this."

Jack self-consciously pushed the notebook to the side of the table furthest away from Kevin.

"Sorry, dude, but you've been in and out of that thing all night, and the more you won't tell me what the hell you're doing, the more I want to know. I mean, damn, what's going on? Are you plotting a murder or something? Making a to-do list? Writing a song? What's the big secret?"

Jack realized that, in order to get Kevin off his back, he was going to have to either leave or give him more information, and he wasn't ready to leave.

"Alright, man, if you must know, I'm just keeping a record of everything that happens to me tonight."

It wasn't a lie. It wasn't the whole truth, but it wasn't a lie. Jack was proud of himself.

"Interesting. Why?"

Jack took a moment to think of a good answer, or at least something that would sound like a good answer.

"I don't know. I got the idea from a friend. She's a scientist and she drinks a lot and one night she wanted to keep a scientific record of everything she thought of or that happened to her when she was out drinking. She called it a Drunk Log."

Kevin leaned back, stared at the ceiling while he pondered Jack's response.

"A scientist, huh? Well, that sort of makes sense, especially if she's an alcoholic. Maybe I should try it one night."

Kevin seemed excited by the idea of his own Drunk Log.

"Maybe you should. But let me warn you ahead of time; if you do try it, all kinds of people will start asking you what you're writing about."

Kevin smiled at Jack's dig.

"I'm sure I can handle it, or at least be better than you are at hiding it."

Kevin's company was again feeling less troublesome than Jack originally feared, so he decided to delay his departure from MOTR yet again.

"Let me buy you a drink, Kevin."

"Nope. These are still on me, Jack What are you having?"

The second band of the evening started playing just as Kevin asked the question, so Jack didn't so much hear it as see the words play out on Kevin's lips. In response, he held up his finger in a wordless request for Kevin to give him a minute to think about it. Kevin complied, waving his understanding back to Jack, then he just stood there, waiting for Jack to make a decision.

"Just a bourbon and coke for me!"

Jack mouthed the words carefully and increased his volume to what he believed was an acceptable level, but it still took three tries before Kevin appeared to understand. His secret out, Jack was no longer trying to hide the log from his pleasant tablemate.

10:17

I know what you're thinking, Posterity.
You think I've spent too much time in this one bar. You think
I'm chickening out.
But don't worry. I'm not. I'll get moving soon enough.
To be honest, though, I'm enjoying Kevin's company,
although I'm not sure why he's so keen on buying me drinks
tonight.
It's not like I'm trying to save money.
I think he's staring at me. I'll check . . .

Yup, he's over in line for drinks but he's still looking over at me.

Does it seem a little creepy? Do you think he maybe has a man-crush on me?

Maybe my hair is messed up? No, for sure my hair is messed up.

It's the hat. And the snow. Jeez! Who gives a crap? What trivial nonsense!

Does anyone care about my hair or my hat? For fuck's sake, I hope not.

"What are you writing?"

Jack's eyes were still aimed downward when he heard the words. He fought the urge to slam his fist on the table in protest before realizing the question came from a new voice, one he did not recognize. So, instead of pounding on the table, he opted for a deep breath before bringing his eyes up from the notebook. The attractive, female bassist from the previous band was standing next to him, smiling.

"Um . . . you know, just keeping track of things."

The band was now playing a softer song, so Jack didn't have to yell.

"I get it. I do it all the time. I keep mine in a gym bag when we're on the road."

Jack was at a loss. He had no idea why this girl with pink hair was talking to him, no idea what criteria she had used to pick him out of the crowd. "Yeah, I just fold mine up and put it in my pocket. Thought I'd look silly carrying a gym bag around all night."

The pink-haired bassist laughed.

"I'm Lucy. Can I buy you a drink?"

Jack scribbled something and closed the log.

Aria and Tracy drank their wine in near silence. Tracy knew Aria was withholding something important, and Aria knew that Tracy knew, but neither was willing to broach the topic, whatever that topic might be. At least not yet. Until one of them was ready to crack, they made small talk and allowed the conversations of others in the packed bar to interrupt their own. Though it was already busy when the two walked in, Liberty's had grown busier, and was now full to capacity. Tracy and Aria were surrounded by bodies, which was making Tracy anxious. For her part, Aria was used to the crowd, albeit from the safety of the other side of the bar. Tracy tried to distract herself from the jostling crowd by leaning in close and engaging her friend.

"Hey, let's try this again. I want to talk about what's going on with you."

Aria looked at Tracy and rolled her eyes, as if that should send the message that it was much too loud to discuss anything at all. Tracy didn't take notice and continued.

"I feel like there's something weird going on with you tonight."

Aria took a moment before deciding it was time to acquiesce.

"If I tell you, you're going to think I'm a nut job."

"So what? I already think that. Spill it."

Aria proceeded to tell her friend everything that had happened with Jack up until that point. Tracy listened intently, asking the occasional question. When Aria was done describing her travels and her reasons behind them, Tracy looked her in the eye.

"So, this is about Steffi."

It was not a question. It was an observation.

"Okay, fine. It's about Steffi, but it's also about Jack." Aria paused to give herself time to think about what she just said. "I'm afraid Jack is going to hurt himself."

"Because of the notebook."

"Yes. Like I said, he was here earlier tonight, while I was working, writing in a notebook. I 'accidentally' read some of what he was writing."

Aria was embarrassed to admit her intrusion into Jack's thoughts, but she figured if she was going to come clean with Tracy, she may as well tell her everything. The cat was out of the bag.

Tracy thought for a minute, took a sip of wine, and looked out the window at the falling snow.

"So, you've been trying to find him all night."

"Yes, pretty much."

Having confessed, Aria felt a weight beginning to lift.

Tracy looked at her friend, lifted her glass of wine. "Well, I've got nothing better to do. We'd best get moving."

"Yeah?"

"Let's do it. Cheers."

Chapter Fourteen

Missed Him By This Much, Redux

The wheels of the gurney snapped to the ground as Jack was rolled out of the ambulance. Jesse was still there. Jack could see his face floating above him. He knew he was at a hospital, but he didn't know which one. There was a doctor asking him if he knew his name and the day of the week. Jack remembered his name but couldn't remember what day it was. He wondered how all of this could have happened in just a single day, in just a moment, really, if he believed it at all.

> *10:34*
> *Hold on a second, Posterity.*
> *For some reason, there's a hot, hippie musician with pink hair, asking me if I want a drink.*
> *I should keep writing but that would be rude, I think. I'm not sure.*
> *Is there a guidebook for this sort of thing, or some precedent I should be following?*
> *Here's what I'm going to do . . .*
> *I'm going to talk to her for a minute and get back to you.*

"Uh, sure. I'd love that."

Jack set the pen down as he looked at his new acquaintance. He had not forgotten Kevin, who was already in the process of getting him a drink, but somehow was unable, or unwilling, to relate that information to the pale bassist.

"I'm Jack, by the way."

"I'm Lucy. What are you drinking?"

Lucy was relaxed, almost as if she took drink orders from strangers for a living.

"Hmm. I'll have whatever you're having."

Lucy released a small laugh.

"That's risky. What if I get one of those things with an umbrella?"

"Well, you don't really look like the umbrella type. Besides, I'm not sure they know how to make those in this place."

Lucy reached out to touch Jack's shoulder before taking a step toward the bar. Once her back was turned, Jack took the opportunity to find Kevin, who was still in line for drinks, but further down the bar from Lucy. Kevin's eyes had been on Jack during the entire encounter with Lucy, and he was now holding his arms in a shrug, silently asking Jack an important, existential question.

"What the hell are you doing?"

Jack shrugged his shoulders back at Kevin, thereby relieving himself of any responsibility for the encounter with Lucy the Bassist. Meanwhile, Lucy, who happened to be much prettier than Kevin, was already getting served by one of the male bartenders.

10:41

Still short on time, Posterity.

The musician is getting us drinks, even as we speak.

Here's the problem: I can't figure out why the universe has put this girl in my way,

especially now.

What am I supposed to do here? Trade phone numbers?

No, that wouldn't make any sense unless I was just trying to get rid of her.

Besides, wouldn't that sort of be cheating?
I think you know what I'm talking about, Posterity.
In the end though, in the grand scheme of things, it doesn't matter.
Still, I suppose it's nice to be noticed.
Okay—I have to stop writing now because she is setting drinks down on the table.
I'm going to look ungrateful if I don't stop.

"Thanks for this, Lucy."

The two shots of tequila Lucy purchased for herself and Jack were now sitting in front of him, as were two slices of lime. Jack reflexively searched for a salt shaker, but failed to locate one.

"You're welcome, Jack."

Lucy reached behind her and grabbed a salt shaker from the bar.

"Are you looking for this?"

"I am." Jack could still see Kevin ordering drinks and started to panic.

"Can I ask you a question?"

"Before we do shots?"

Lucy had a wry, amused look on her face.

"Sure, Jack. Go for it."

"Not to sound unconfident, or needy, but what brought you over to my table?"

Jack wasn't sure 'unconfident' was even a real word, but couldn't think of a viable substitute in the time allotted.

"Oh, I don't know." Lucy took the half step required to bring her close enough to speak right into Jack's ear. She smelled heavenly, despite having performed on a hot stage for the last forty minutes. "I suppose it's because when I got offstage, I looked over here and saw you writing by yourself in the middle of a crowd of people. I thought that was weird and figured you could use some company, even if you didn't think you wanted any."

"I'm not sure how to respond to that, as much as I'd like to. So, I think I'm going to blame the alcohol."

"For what?"

"For everything."

Jack dragged the lime slice across the space between his thumb and forefinger and shook salt on it while Lucy did the same.

"What are we drinking to? World peace?"

Lucy laughed.

"Funny, Jack. How about we drink to . . . keeping a record? To remembering."

Jack was not inclined to explain to Lucy that one of his goals that evening was to actually forget, even though he knew it wouldn't happen, no matter how much he drank. Still, he understood where she was coming from. She kept her own log, though hers was full of song snippets and half-completed poems, or so he imagined. She was a musician, after all.

"Here's to playing in a band."

Jack lifted the shot glass from the table.

"That's good enough for me."

She emptied her glass and Jack followed suit.

"Thanks for this, Lucy."

By now Kevin was hovering behind Lucy, holding two drinks, apparently not wanting to interrupt whatever chemistry was brewing right in front of him.

"My pleasure, Jack."

Lucy put her hand back on Jack's shoulder.

"Listen, I'm going to be around the bar for a while. Come talk to me if you feel like it."

"I will."

Jack said the words but doubted that he would. While the encounter was pleasant and unexpected, he felt vaguely guilty about flirting with her. As she walked away, Jack motioned to Kevin that it was okay to return to the table.

"What was that about?"

"Not sure. Pity shots, I think."

"Hmm, let's see, Jack. Is it possible you're radiating something? Despair, maybe?"

Kevin sat down across the table. "You want to get out of here? I don't like this band."

To Jack, Kevin's question sounded odd for two reasons, the first being that the two had never spent any time together outside of MOTR. The second that he just handed Jack a drink and still had one for himself.

"Um, sure, Kevin. Let's get out of here."

Though he recognized his own voice, Jack had no idea from what part of him the words were coming. Before he could give it a thought, he downed his drink as fast as he could while Kevin did the same.

"Awesome. Follow me." Kevin, having finished his drink, was already moving, wrapping himself in his scarf and jacket whilst traversing the three yards to the door. "Damn! Look at the snow!"

Tracy stood at the bar, waiting to pay the bill, while Aria gave some thought to where they should next venture. She had already covered the entire area between Main and Vine, and so believed they should cover Race and Elm, too. It wouldn't take much time. On those streets there were only a few bars from which to choose. *But then what?* She wondered. *Should I give up at that point?*

The thought of quitting made her anxious. Up until that moment, she had not spent any time considering a scenario in which she did *not* find Jack, but what had made her so sure she would be successful in the first place? Had she really just gone blindly into the night, hoping for the best? She could only think that must be the truth. She had thrown herself blindly into the quest, into the search for Jack. She was responsible. She was colluding only with herself, until now.

"You ready to go?"

Tracy startled Aria out of her contemplation.

"Uh, yeah, sure. Absolutely. Thanks, Tracy."

Aria had never offered a more sincere "thanks" in her life.

"Are you sure you're going to be okay in those shoes? It's going to be slippery."

"I'll be fine, sweetie. Let's get this show on the road."

Tracy led the way through the churning pack of humanity blocking their exit. They were only a few yards from the door but the journey, fraught with excuse-me-pleases and sorries, seemed to last an age. Finally, they were outside, surrounded by snowflakes and able to take a deep breath.

"Which way?"

Aria had decided, sometime between the initial onset of anxiousness and Tracy's return from paying their tab, that she had no choice but to complete the grid, which meant checking out the bars on Race Street and Elm. She knew that she might be wasting her time, and that she might be better served by again trolling the bars on Vine and Main. Either way, she knew it was a crapshoot.

"That way."

Aria pointed south toward 14th Street, the shortest route to Elm. They turned and walked south, Tracy moving gingerly on the slippery side-walk. Aria, whose hiking boots afforded her a good deal more traction than Tracy's attractive, but less-than-practical, three-inch boot heels, took notice of Tracy's struggles, and locked arms with her to provide support. Arm in arm they picked through the snow to the intersection of 14th and Main and, once upon it, should have turned right. But Aria was having another vision. The vision, which formed about halfway down the block. Took the form of Jack, and was emerging from MOTR with another man, one whom she did not recognize. Initially Aria did not believe what she was seeing, and froze in place to get a better look. Enthralled by the possibility she had finally found Jack, she ignored Tracy, who was tugging at her arm. Finally, after daring herself to believe it really was Jack, she called out to him.

"Jack!"

Aria yelled his name but he showed no sign of having heard her, the wind suppressing the tenor and volume of her voice.

She yelled again.

"Jack!"

When Jack still did not seem to hear her calling for him, Aria instinctively stepped toward him, but felt herself restrained by Tracy, who was still holding onto Aria for dear life.

"Is that him?"

Tracy was trying to make herself heard over Aria's yelling.

"Yes, yes. That's him, Tracy. I have to get to him."

As gently and urgently as she could, Aria extricated her arm from Tracy's and took a giant stride toward MOTR.

This is it!

Disaster struck.

Though Aria's hiking boots did, indeed, provided the sure footing she could never have enjoyed with normal street shoes, let alone four-inch heels, they failed to provide her with the x-ray vision necessary to peer through the fallen snow to see the icy, hidden curb below. It was this hidden curb, buried beneath the early-season snowfall, that reached out to grab Aria's foot as she attempted her leap of faith. It was this hidden curb on which she only partially set her foot down, half on and half off. The resulting imbalance between heel and forefoot brought Aria down onto the snow and pavement.

In fact, Aria fell so hard and so fast it made Tracy scream at the sight of it. Aria did not hear Tracy's scream. Instead, the last thing Aria heard, before her head hit the pavement, was the combined sound of locking brakes and a screeching car horn. The next thing she heard was her friend's voice.

"Damn it, Aria! Are you okay?"

Tracy kneeled beside Aria, cradling her head in her hands. A strange man hovered behind her. Aria assumed he was the driver of the car, whose progress she had impeded.

"Can you get up?"

"Yeah, I'm good, Tracy. Thanks."

Tracy, with the help of the friendly, stranded driver, got Aria to her feet in short order and moved her out of the intersection.

"Thanks, guys. I'm good."

She gently shook herself loose from the supportive hands of her friend and the driver, who had been kind enough not to kill her.

"What the hell, Aria? Are you trying to kill yourself?"

Tracy was rattled by the sight of her friend almost getting run over. Aria felt her hands shaking as they attempted to regrip Aria, as if this time she was the one providing stability. "Okay, now what?"

Tracy was referring to the flashing police lights bearing down on them. No siren, just lights. Unbeknownst to Tracy and Aria, the police-woman about to render assistance had been stuck at a stop sign ten yards away, watching the scene unfold.

"Is everything okay here, ladies?"

The officer assumed, from her initial vantage point, she was dealing with yet another garden variety, drunk-on-a-Friday-night situation.

"I'm fine, ma'am. We're fine, I mean. Yeah, I just tripped. I didn't see the curb because of the snow."

Aria was impatient. Every moment spent dealing with the authorities put her further off Jack's tail. She glanced down the street, hoping he might be loitering in front of MOTR but had no such luck. Her heart sank. She had been so close.

"Ma'am, you're bleeding. Why don't you let me get someone over here to check that out?"

"I'm sorry, officer, but I really don't have time."

Aria took a step toward MOTR but was restrained by Tracy, now holding her arm with an iron grip.

"For God's sake, Aria. You're bleeding. Let someone check you out. You might have a concussion. I should take you to the hospital."

Aria tried to pry herself free, but Tracy would not release her.

"You should listen to your friend, ma'am. I can have somebody over here in a few minutes, unless you want to go to the emergency room. Better safe than sorry."

Aria closed her eyes and tried to, unsuccessfully, wish her predicament away. When she opened her eyes, she did her best to peer into the back seat of the police car, hoping, through some miracle, she might find Jack sitting in the back seat.

By that point, the officer had decided that Aria and Tracy were not drunk, or at least not very drunk. They were just impatient. While this boded well from a time-wasted-getting-a-sobriety-check perspective, Aria was still in a pickle. Jack was getting away, but her friend was not going to let her move until she allowed a professional to examine her bleeding head, which she hadn't even noticed until the cop and Tracy pointed it out. She wasn't exactly sure how much time and money ambulance medics would cost her, but she knew a trip to the emergency room would take hours, at least.

"Okay. Fine. Call the paramedics, please."

Jack and Kevin were aware of the blue, flashing lights illuminating the buildings around them but paid them little attention. It was, at least, the third time either of them had been confronted with sirens or lights that evening. Flashing lights of one kind or another were a ubiquitous backdrop to the entire neighborhood. The fellow travelers paid them little attention, not bothering to see from which direction they were emanating or why they were emanating at all. Whatever it was would be taken care of by the person in charge of the psychedelic light show.

"Where to?"

Kevin's voice reminded Jack that he was on his way to somewhere. Kevin was matter of fact about the situation. To the best of his knowledge, there was no overriding plan guiding their movements. He just figured his newly minted drinking buddy had been as ready to leave MOTR as he was and, duly prompted, was eager to explore a different watering hole.

"Let's head toward the river. Plenty of bars down the street."

Jack was matter of fact as well. He wasn't letting Kevin in on his little plan and, despite the fact he was enjoying Kevin's company, knew he'd have to ditch him before he got too close to the river.

"Sounds good."

The blue police lights faded as they waded further south, and by the time the paramedics added their red lights to the ocular cacophony, they didn't register at all. Jack kept a brisk pace despite the alcohol and the chronic soreness in his hip. He felt no real sense of urgency, as he was sure of the inevitable outcome of his trip to the river, but still couldn't slow himself down for fear he might change his mind, or maybe get too lazy to make the final move.

Within a few minutes, he and Kevin reached Central Parkway, the edge of the neighborhood and a turning point for Jack.

"Sorry, Trace. I'm okay."

Aria managed to squeeze the apology out from behind the latex-gloved hands of the paramedic, who had already cleaned the gash on her forehead and was applying butterfly bandages to pull the skin together. Tracy had said little since the paramedics arrived, and was now just standing in the snow, shivering as she watched Aria get patched up.

"Are you? Really? You're acting like a nut case, Aria. I mean, I think I get what you're trying to do. But, for God's sake, there's gotta be a limit."

The paramedic broke into their conversation.

"Uh, if I can interject, you might still want to think about going to the hospital for stitches. I think these will work but it couldn't hurt to take the trip."

"Thank you, Connor."

Aria had read his name tag when he first arrived. There was a lady paramedic as well, but she was in the truck on the radio, apparently getting instructions on their next destination.

"I'm sure it's fine."

"Okay, then. For what it's worth, I don't think you have a concussion, but that's something you might want to get checked out by your doctor."

Paramedic Connor completed the work on Aria's head and began repacking his tackle box, which was chock-full of bandages, tape, scissors, and all manner of emergency medical gear, which he would probably use up by the end of the night. Friday nights had a habit of doing that in this part of Cincinnati.

The police officer, who had waited patiently with Aria and Tracy for the paramedic to arrive, had Aria sign a piece of paper on a clipboard and made her goodbyes. Paramedic Connor had his own paper and clipboard and, after Aria signed his, drove away with his partner. Tracy and Aria, having been an object of curiosity for many bar hoppers and passersby over the last half hour, were now left alone to stare at each other, being kept company only by boring, white streetlamps.

"What now?"

"I don't know, Tracy. I think I'm actually going to go home."

Aria was lying, but Tracy was cold enough to want to believe her.

"Thank God! I thought we might be out here all night!"

The fact that Tracy had been willing to join Aria on her quest, especially in the face of the weather, the accident, and her unfortunate choice of footwear, brought tears of gratitude to Aria's eyes. She tucked Tracy's arm under hers and walked her to her car, just a block away.

"Aria, are you going to be okay? Why don't you let me drive you home?"

"I'm fine, Trace. It's only a couple blocks."

"Trade me coats."

"What? Mine is fine, Trace."

"No, it's not. It's wet through and you're shivering. Mine's in better shape. Trade me and we can trade back tomorrow. I insist."

Aria relented and made the trade, surprised Tracy's coat really was warmer than her own. One more hug and Tracy gently pulled her car into the street, now devoid of traffic. Aria watched her drive away, making sure she stayed put long enough to be invisible to Tracy's rear-view mirror before turning to make her way to MOTR.

Chapter Fifteen

Bar Fight, Redux

Jack drifted into consciousness. He was cold. He could see his blanket-covered body and couldn't understand why he was so cold. He felt disoriented, but not in an unpleasant way, and he could see two or three needles had been taped to his hands. There were tubes attached to the needles, at least one of which was pumping pain killers into his system. There were people standing around his bed. There were at least as many people as there were needles and tubes in his hand. They were talking, but not to him. For now, the accident seemed a distant memory. He was able to relax for the first time in what seemed like hours. Jack drifted in and out and then out, again.

11:14
I'm hiding in a port-o-potty behind a taco truck.
I'm in the dark, basically. I'm writing in the dark. There's just enough light to stay in the lines.
Kevin said he was hungry and the taco truck almost showed up out of nowhere,
like it showed up just to feed Kevin.
It's snowing pretty hard and I didn't think it was a good idea to try to write in the snow, so I ducked in here.
Off topic - this would be a good place to do drugs. It's private and it's got a lock.
Even better than a crack house. I'll bet people shoot up in these things.

I would, if I were a drug addict.

This is what I am now—a guy that writes in a notebook in a portable bathroom.

Any bathroom will do, I guess.

This is what I am now.

I'm pretty drunk, Posterity, so you should be impressed with my writing ability right about now.

I'm working really hard to keep this legible.

Walking in the snow sobered me up a little. But not too much.

I'm feeling the beer courage starting to rumble.

Hell, the pink-haired girl (Lucy) proved that.

I've never been that good at talking to girls, unless I know them.

I actually went for a few minutes without thinking about Troy.

I've done five minutes before. I was pretty drunk then, too.

Problem is, when I don't think about him, I feel guilty for that too.

There's no way out of this.

Well, that's not true.

That's about it for this bathroom break. Sorry about the sloppy writing.

Can't be helped.

Jack folded the notebook and, ever so carefully, slid it into his back pocket. It would be disastrous if it fell into the part of the port-o-potty from which it would be rendered irretrievable. After double checking to make sure the log was as deep as it would go in his pocket, Jack adjusted his pea coat, made sure that no part of the notebook would be exposed to the storm. When he exited, he found Kevin standing on the sidewalk, finishing off the remainder of his street tacos, lost in thought.

"Thanks for waiting."

Kevin turned to Jack, still chewing.

"No problem, dude. The snow's beautiful, huh?"

"It is. Definitely."

"Where to?"

Jack had given their next bar some thought. Bathrooms weren't just for writing. A person can get a lot of thinking done in a bathroom, especially in a snowstorm.

"Let's go to the Main Event."

Kevin stopped chewing.

"Really?"

Jack looked up and shrugged.

"Really."

The Main Event was the reincarnation of a gay bar called The Subway. About a decade before, The Subway and all the residents who lived in the flop house that existed above it had been kicked out of a building on Walnut Street to make room for a high-end hotel. Once evicted, the denizens of the flop house scattered to the four winds, as by then the city was running out of flop houses. However, The Subway, having thus far been a successful concern, chose not to gracefully fade into the darkness, and moved a couple blocks away, to be reborn as the Main Event.

Though the new place was every bit as dilapidated as its predecessor, it no longer had a reputation as a straight-friendly gay bar, though some vestiges of that history remained, like the occasional drag show playing out on the huge dance floor. Nowadays, the Main Event's weekday patrons frequently consisted of an eclectic group of local panhandlers, drug dealers and, most likely, the occasional prostitute. Though the dirty facade was usually enough to warn most "regular" people away on weekdays, the occasional hearty traveler or intrepid downtowner could be found inside. Conversely, the weekend crowd included people of all stripes, sizes, shapes, and socioeconomic situations.

Jack chose the Main Event on purpose. He chose it because he needed to get rid of Kevin before he got to the river and was hoping the seediness of the place would be sufficiently overwhelming to Kevin's gentle psyche that he would choose to abandon Jack of his own accord. Kevin's reaction to the mere suggestion of walking into the Main Event let Jack know he made the right decision about what was likely to be the last bar visit of his life.

Kevin, for his part, was quietly questioning all the decisions he had made leading him to this place, a joint he had been inside only once before and felt no compunction to revisit. He was kicking himself, thinking he could have just stayed at MOTR, as usual, hung out by himself, as usual, and gone home alone, as usual.

"Okay. Whatever. I guess."

Kevin could see the place. It was only a block away.

"Excuse me."

Aria approached the bouncer at MOTR, although she wasn't sure the job of sitting beside a door and asking patrons for their driver's licenses was still categorized as "bouncer." Door guy? Security guy? She didn't have time to find out.

"What's up? Hey, don't you work up the street? At Libs?"

"Uh, yes, I do."

"How do you like it over there?"

This . . . whatever his title might be, is already too chatty, Aria thought. She needed to keep moving.

"It's good. It's good. Hey, do you know a guy named Jack? I think he was here earlier."

"Jack? The regular? Kinda tall? I think so. How come? And what happened to your head? Looks bad."

Clearly, the Bouncer/Security Guy did not share Aria's sense of urgency. An influx of patrons suddenly streamed around her, all of them trying to shove their licenses into the Bouncer/ID Inspector's hands for his perusal. But he seemed perfectly fine talking to Aria, barely glancing at the plastic cards stacking up in his hand.

"Just wondering if you saw which way he went when he left?"

"I think I saw him go down Main, you know, toward the river. He was with that other guy. I think his name is Kevin. Do you know him? Jeez! Did you get stitches?"

"Okay, thanks!"

Aria was back out the door and into the snow, hoping she hadn't been too rude, but then didn't really care. She was on a mission. In this case, manners were not a priority.

Aria's head throbbed and the wind blew directly in her face, but she ignored both as merely inconvenient. She was excited, more hopeful than she had been all night, despite the medical delay at the corner. She had convinced herself that Jack would not stray from his southerly course, that he would remain on a straight line until he got to wherever he was going.

Where is he? Where? Where? Where?

Being careful in the snow, Aria walked as fast as she could in the snow without risking more danger to life or limb. After all, she had already fallen twice that evening, and though she didn't know it, she would fall once more. As she plunged further into the storm, she thought of how late it was getting, how close she had been to Jack before she fell and, unexpectedly, how her sister might have felt in the hours before she took her own life.

Fear drove her into the storm.

The snow on the sidewalk disguised a growing layer of ice beneath, making every step difficult and tiring her legs.

She was stopped by a traffic light a block short of the edge of Over the Rhine. While waiting for two cars to skid their way through the intersection, the feeling of being stalked returned.

Aria thought back to the last time she had spoken with her sister. It was three days before she killed herself. She sounded fine on the phone. Ostensibly, Steffi called Aria just to say hello, to "check in" in her own words, and to see what her big sister was up to at college. They chatted for at least half an hour, and Aria's impression after the phone call was that she couldn't remember the last time her sister sounded so calm. This should have been cause for joy but, for some reason, only made Aria apprehensive.

She knew now, after multiple rounds of therapy following Steffi's death, that her sister *was* calm; that the reason she was calm was that she had already decided to kill herself. In that phase, Steffi was, essentially, making the rounds of family and friends to say goodbye, without actually using the word. Aria would never forgive herself for missing it. She would never forgive herself for not calling her mother or father, for allowing herself to think her sister was alright even when she suspected she wasn't.

Of course, everyone told Aria it wasn't her fault, which it wasn't; that everyone else seemed to miss the signs as well, which they had. But still, for many months Aria couldn't shake the feeling she had missed something, something in that last conversation that was different from their other conversations, something that had nothing to do with Steffi's tranquil tone.

It was years later, years spent replaying their last conversation over and over again in her mind, that the difference was revealed. It was this: Steffi never mentioned joining Aria at college. For Steffi, joining her sister at college had become an article of faith, evidently a lifeline that helped her lurch through one bad day to the next; that helped her hang on. It was something to which she could look forward as a new beginning. The sisters rarely had an exchange during Aria's last year in high school and through her first semester in college during which Steffi did not mention her own matriculation and the chance to be reunited with her big sister. That was the thing Aria had missed, the thing that stuck with her every day, the thing that wouldn't disappear.

Standing on the corner, lashed by wind and snow, Aria knew she could not ignore what was happening with Jack, that she couldn't allow herself to ignore the voice inside telling her something was very wrong. It fell upon her to try and do something about it. She had ignored the voice before, and her entire life since that moment had been forever altered. It had been transformed to the point she hid from the world, ensconced behind two feet of wood, in a job which did not require the degree she eventually earned.

I will find him.

Aria reached Central Parkway, just about to leave the neighborhood. She heard the sirens while she waited for the walk signal, and then came the lights. They were converging just a couple blocks ahead of her. She was getting closer.

Despite Kevin's trepidation or, more likely, because of it, Jack was forced to shove him through the entrance door of the Main Event. Indeed, they had hovered in front of it for almost a minute, Kevin frozen in place, unwilling or unable to enter.

Jack wanted to give him a moment to acclimate, but the storm swirling around them forced him to take matters into his own hands, specifically Kevin, who did not object to being manhandled, and who breathed a sigh of relief once he was through the door and able to observe the place was not (yet) full of knife-wielding thugs and ne'er-do-wells.

For Jack, the crowd wasn't nearly as sleazy as he had hoped. While some of the patrons were assuredly occupying the lower rungs of the economic ladder, most of the drinkers came across as an average Friday night bar crowd, which was disappointing. He hadn't chosen the Main Event because he thought Kevin would like it. He chose it because he hoped Kevin would *not,* thereby creating an opportunity to gently nudge him out of his current orbit for the evening or, for that matter, for the rest of his life.

Jack decided to order drinks and give the place a chance to live down to his expectations.

"What are you having, Kevin? It's on me."

Kevin, having regained his composure since his unceremonious entrance moments before, was examining the drink menu, plastic covered and a tad grimy.

"Hmm . . . well, if you're buying, I'll have a single malt, neat."

"Good choice."

Jack couldn't recall Kevin ever drinking anything other than beer, though admittedly the total time he spent with Kevin, including that evening, was most likely no more than fifteen or twenty hours, accumulated over the two years they had been acquainted at MOTR.

Jack ordered two scotches and looked around. The crowd, fairly substantial, was mostly congregating on the outskirts of the dance floor, which was lit with stage lights suspended from the ceiling. Jack checked his watch. It was definitely late enough for a drag show, should there be one scheduled, and this would explain the bright lights and hopeful anticipation exuding from the crowd.

Jack's musings were interrupted by the bartender delivering the drinks.

"Is there a show tonight?"

The bartender seemed pleasant enough.

"Starts any minute now."

Jack was excited to give Kevin the news.

"There's a show tonight."

"Really? What kind of show?"

"Drag."

"Really? A drag show? I've never been to one."

Kevin seemed genuinely excited, meaning Jack's plan was failing, rather spectacularly, so far. Then again, the show hadn't started yet. Still, Kevin was having too good of a time. Jack was going to have to be more creative or, perhaps, more caustic and mean.

Jack's initial idea, to desert Kevin inside Main Event, should be easy enough to pull off once the show started. Once enraptured by the show, Kevin's focus would be off Jack, and he could just slip away. The more he thought about it the more he liked the simplicity. Kevin's feelings would most likely be hurt, but only for a few hours. Certainly, news of Jack's watery death would adequately distract him from his bruised ego.

When the house lights went down, Jack and Kevin wandered into the crowd. Moments later a disembodied voice boomed through the speakers, letting the throng know the show was about to start, along with the names of the featured performers. A Cher song began just as the dance floor lights were brought up and, as if by magic, the first performer of the night, Queen Bee, appeared in the center of the dance floor.

Queen Bee's physique, it should be noted, was reminiscent of an NFL linebacker which, it turned out, she had actually been in a previous incarnation. Though she did a decent job of lip syncing to Cher's "If I Could Turn Back Time," and her costume superbly elaborate, her dance moves left something to be desired. This mattered little to the audience in general and, excluding a familiar looking knot of younger drinkers hovering just off the dance floor, Queen Bee's act was greeted with cheers and applause.

Having never been to a drag show, Kevin was appropriately rapt, and found himself drawn to the dance floor. This served to create some separation between him and his drinking buddy, which pleased Jack. Distance was his friend, as it would help enable a quiet exit. He just had to plan it so that he would be granted the most time possible to get away before Kevin noticed his absence. To that end, he decided to wait for the next performer to begin, but the next performance would be delayed.

The trouble started with the knot of younger drinkers, likely uninitiated to drag show etiquette, and definitely very drunk by the time the show started. Jack remembered them as his "friends" from Vestry, and was surprised the police had allowed them to continue to roam free through the city.

As the applause diminished, a young man's voice came to the fore.

"Yeah, nice job, Queen Bee! Great dance moves."

His comment, though mostly innocuous, did not please the Queen. Nor did the laughter of the young man's cohorts. Queen Bee, whose given name was David Sandler, had had a rough day. Queen Bee/David Sandler lived in Blue Ash, a suburb of the city, and had to fight the snow and traffic just to show up that night. It was her first show ever, a fact that likely made her a little more sensitive than usual. Add to that the stress that came with lying to his wife and teenage children about his newfound hobby, not to mention his whereabouts in the middle of a snowstorm, and you had the makings of a time bomb, one which exploded quickly and furiously.

Before the young man and his friends knew what was happening, Queen Bee had thrown herself into the lot of them, using all the training he had gleaned from his years playing football. In one moment, the mouthy young man and his friends were on their feet, laughing at a heavyset drag queen, in the next they found themselves sprawled out on the floor, piled on top of one another, taken out en masse by a man in a dress.

These frat boys tangled with the wrong dude.

The melee escalated when those who had been tackled recovered enough to fight back, which they did. But now they weren't just fighting Queen Bee. They were up against all the other performers as well who, in solidarity with the Queen, had emerged from the dressing room out in a sort of bench clearing brawl. Within moments, nearly everyone in the bar got sucked into the disturbance, including Jack and Kevin, who had each suffered a blow or two at the outset but were now trying to extricate themselves from the morass.

Jack, with more experience at this sort of thing, recovered his footing before Kevin, and decided to use the bar fight to his benefit. Though the house lights were still down, he could spy Kevin taking cover in an opposite corner and took advantage of the confusion to slip outside. He was confident Kevin didn't see him leave because his attention was, by necessity, turned elsewhere to take care of his own survival. Though he knew it had to be done, Jack felt a pang of guilt for deserting Kevin. He had been a good friend that night.

From three blocks away, Aria saw the flashing lights of police vehicles gathering in front of the Main Event. Though she couldn't tell exactly which bar was the cause of the ruckus, she took it as a sign that she was on the right track.

She couldn't know if Jack would be there or not, but hoped he was part of whatever was going on, as long as he didn't end up arrested or anything like that.

If he was there, she thought, he might be in handcuffs, or perhaps injured, even ever so slightly, and if that was the case he would be slowed down enough for her to catch up. Aria figured she could use any assist she could get.

Nearing the Main Event, she could see people milling about on the sidewalk and street, interacting with each other and with the cops, who were still sorting out the details of the bar fight that had occurred barely twenty minutes ago.

Please. Please. Please.

"Excuse me, sir."

Aria bravely approached an officer who was in the middle of taking a statement from one of the accidental participants to the fight. The officer did not appreciate the interruption and looked at her as if she were just another annoyance. "By any chance, have you talked to a guy named Jack?"

"No ma'am. And I'm in the middle of something here. Maybe go inside and ask around."

The person the officer was interviewing spoke up.

"Wait, you're looking for Jack? Jack the engineer?"

Kevin was proud of himself for remembering Jack's profession.

Aria didn't recognized Kevin. He did not frequent Liberty's.

"I am. Yes! Do you know him?"

"Yeah. He was here a few minutes ago. Does he know you're looking for him?"

"But he's not here now? Do you have any idea where he was going?"

Aria deftly avoided Kevin's second question, although she was prepared to lie should it have become necessary.

"No, I think he ducked out when the fight started."

Kevin had received at least one good blow. A knot was growing above his left eye. He kept touching it reflexively as he spoke with the cop and Aria.

"I'm not sure where he was going, but if I had to guess, I'd say toward the river."

Aria's heart leapt.

I'm close.

"Thank you so much and . . . good luck."

"If you see him, tell him I'm pissed."

Kevin's words were directed at Aria's back. She was already ten feet away and moving as fast as the snow and ice would allow.

Chapter Sixteen

The End Is Nigh

When Jack regained consciousness, he was still surrounded by people, but this time, he knew them. His mother, father, and brother were all there. He would find out later that his sister-in-law refused to come into his room. His parents confirmed Troy was dead, and cried with him before they left. While they were in his room, they did not offer their forgiveness, his mother never would. Jack agreed with his mother. He wouldn't forgive himself either.

11:42

Wow. Another bar fight? Who'd have thought that could happen?

It worked out for me, though, and Kevin too, if you think about it.

So where in the world am I?

At the moment I'm standing under the canopy of a restaurant that closed a few hours ago.

It's protecting me and the log from the snow. Doing a pretty nice job, actually.

Don't know why I didn't think of this earlier.

There's nobody out now. No one to interrupt me.

Posterity, you might think I'm sad right now, you know, because I'm planning to kill myself and all,

but know this, I'm actually feeling really good, and it's not just the alcohol.

I feel like I'm setting myself free.
I've been haunted for a year and it will finally be over.
I feel like I am just a hair away from freedom.
It's been so long since I felt . . . unburdened. But soon it will all be over.
I'd like to think I'll see Troy again, but we'll have to see which religion has got that one right,
you know, considering the suicide and all.
If it's up to the Christians, I'm going right to hell.
The Buddhists might have something else to say.
Still, I'd like to see him, and ask him to forgive me.
He's a kid. He might still have it in him.

Jack folded the notebook and slipped it back into his rear pocket, pleased with how full it looked when he had it open. He took a minute to look at the snow. He couldn't remember ever seeing a snowstorm like that so early in the season. It wasn't even Thanksgiving yet.

Part of him wanted to just stand and enjoy the beauty of it, while another part wanted to get back out into it, to finish the job. He let the first part win, for a moment. His hip was bothering him anyway, making it easier to remain for a while in the relatively snow-free area under the canopy, watching his footprints disappear. He was only ten minutes or so from the bridge, after all, even with the meteorological shenanigans impeding his progress.

Finally, Jack stepped out into the snow. He wasn't more than two blocks from the Main Event and didn't want to be spotted by Kevin or the cops, or anyone hovering around the scene of the crime, so he stayed close to the buildings, his left leg dragging ever so slightly as he strode through the snow. Moments later, he was standing in front of the Bay Horse, a tiny bar a couple blocks south of the Main Event.

Jack decided to duck in for a shot, though he didn't really need it. Indeed. Jack's blood alcohol level was nearly perfect, depending on what kind of test was administered.

Why not have a shot, he asked himself. *Couldn't hurt and wouldn't take any time at all.*

Other than one other man at the bar, whom he did not recognize, Jack had the place to himself.

"What can I get for you?"

The bartender had been playing on his phone before Jack interrupted him.

"Shot of Bushmills, please."

Jack drank, paid, and was back outside in less than two minutes.

Aria picked her way through the snow, knowing she was potentially twenty or thirty minutes behind Jack. Though her confidence was tolerably irrational, still she knew she would find him. She also knew that, if she was wrong, if she should not find him, she would give up once she reached the river. She was not going to chase him endlessly through a storm. She knew, she told herself, that eventually she would have to quit, go home, and hope for the best. But she was so close. By now, she felt Jack so close she could almost reach out and touch him. So, when her phone rang, her mind raced with anticipation.

It was her mother.

"Hello?"

Her first instinct was to not answer. The phone call would slow her down. But then the idea that Tracy might have ratted her out sprang into her head, so she stopped under the canopy of a closed restaurant to take the call.

"Aria. What's going on, dear? Tracy called me a little while ago and told me that you and I needed to talk."

"Not much, Mom. What's going on with you?"

Aria deflected. Her mother sounded concerned, but not overly so. Tracy hadn't clued her in to everything her daughter was up to, or else she would already be at her doorstep. Now was a good time to lie.

"Everything's fine here, sweetie. Why would Tracy tell me to call you?"

Aria forced a giggle.

"I don't know, Mom. I may have gotten a little too drunk earlier?"

It was a good lie. She worked in a bar, after all.

"We met up in that bar behind Kaze and hung out for a while. We did a couple shots, I think. Maybe she got a little worried . . . and drunk, too."

"Well how are you feeling now? And you're not driving, right?"

She knew Aria walked nearly everywhere.

"Better. I took a walk in the snow and I feel better now."

A good lie always has an element of truth.

She smiled at her genius.

"Alright, sweetie. Get some sleep and call me in the morning, okay?"

"Okay, Mom. Goodnight."

Aria took a moment to look around from under the canopy. There was no traffic at all, and whatever sound there might have been was being buried by the snow. Everything around her was perfectly still. Looking down at her boots, she noticed she was standing in someone else's footprints. They were fading in the falling snow, and led south as well, toward the river.

Is their owner limping?

She noticed what she thought might be a slight drag through the snow. If she was going to have any chance of catching Jack, it was time to go.

Stepping back into the storm, it wasn't long before Aria, like Jack just minutes earlier, made it to the Bay Horse. The exterior and interior light flooding onto the sidewalk grabbed her attention, as did the lone customer sitting at the bar.

It was Brian.

Her heart skipped.

This time she was sure. In a moment, she was standing next to him.

"Hi . . . Brian."

"Holy shit. Hi . . . hi, Aria. How are you . . . and what are you doing out in this storm?"

He had seen her come in but didn't believe his eyes until she was standing in front of him.

"Oh, just looking for something. You know . . ."

Her voice trailed off as she stared at him. She didn't know if her inability to draw a breath resulted from the shock of seeing Brian, really seeing Brian, for the first time in years, or if it was the knowledge that she didn't have time to do anything about it.

"Listen, Brian. I know this is a weird place and time to do this, but there's something I've wanted to say to you for a long time.

Brian interrupted.

"Aria, it's okay. Really. It is. I'm okay, and I'm seeing someone, so . . ."

It was Aria's turn to interrupt.

"Brian, I need to tell you how sorry I am, how sorry I *was*, back then. I need you to know that I think about it all time. Can you forgive me?"

Brian smiled at her from his bar stool.

"Of course, Aria. I forgave you a long time ago. Can you forgive me for not being there for you when, well, you know when?"

Aria nodded and threw her arms around him, suddenly ten pounds lighter. She could feel tears welling.

"Thank you, Brian. Thank you."

She kissed him on the cheek and released him from her embrace. "I have to go. I'll call you."

"Wait. What? Aria, can I buy you a drink or something?"

The door swung shut behind her.

The bartender, who had been bored most of the evening, patted himself on the back for staying open during the storm.

Jack left the Bay Horse with the taste of Bushmills still rolling around on his tongue. He was slipping a little on the snow but knew his lack of coordination had nothing to do with the single shot he just polished off. It was, he told himself, the cumulative effect of all the drinks that came before that shot. And the slippery snow, of course. And his tired hip. Were he able to remove any element of that equation, he was sure his gait would straighten right out and any onlookers would be none the wiser.

But there were no onlookers. Jack could see no other humans as he shuffled along. He was greeted only by silent store fronts, falling snow, and streetlights. The streetlights made him feel lonely, standing guard, as they were, over intersections and streets that required no guarding.

Jack kept moving, trying to compose his last log entry, was surprised at his level of ego concerning his last 'words.' He realized, once he started thinking about it, that he wanted them to be profound, like in books and movies, but feared they weren't.

Jack wanted the log to be worth reading, to carry some sort of message that would help people understand, but feared it wouldn't. It occurred to him that the last part, the part about the anger and hurt feelings, might be enough to keep somebody from doing what he was about to do. It occurred to him, not for the first time, the plan, the act itself, was singularly selfish. Jack considered all this already, and kept arriving at the same conclusion—that he didn't deserve to live. He was a murderer, and everyone knew it, but nobody was going to punish him the way he deserved. That being the case, if you want a job done right . . .

But what to write? There was still that. Maybe he would just wing it. He was confident, especially with all the alcohol flowing through his system that, when the pressure was on, he would figure it out, perhaps just before he was to take the leap. After all, he had 'winged it' through about half his classes in college and turned out just fine. *It would come,* he told himself, *the words would come when I need them.*

Lost in these thoughts, Jack heard a sound he did not expect to hear again for the rest of his life. A human voice. He wasn't sure he heard it, until he heard it again.

"Excuse me, Sir. Do you have any money you can spare? I'm really hungry."

Jack stopped walking, looked in the direction of the voice. The owner of the voice was a panhandler, standing by a streetlight in the snow. As far as Jack could tell, the man was not old, but not young, either. It was hard to tell, regardless, given the lighting and his impaired ability to judge much of anything. Jack squinted, trying to get a better look.

"Excuse me, sir. I'm trying to get something to eat."

Jack had to give him credit for his persistence.

"What are you doing out here in the snow?"

The panhandler shrugged his shoulders.

"Man's gotta eat. Can't let a little snow get between me and some food."

Jack nodded and saw a sliver of a smile appear on the man's face. He walked over to him. "Well, tonight is your lucky night, sir."

Had he not been planning to kill himself in the next ten minutes, Jack never would have done what he was about to do. He reached into his back pocket, the one without the log jammed into it, and pulled out whatever cash he had buried in there.

I'm really doing this.

He leafed through the bills.

"A hundred twenty-two dollars. It's all I have."

"Are you sure, sir?"

"Absolutely."

For his efforts, Jack received a hug, and he was fairly sure the man was crying. He gave his new acquaintance a pat on the back, said goodbye and got back on his way.

Aria entered the storm with new hope, feeling almost as if she were floating above the snowy sidewalk. Her elation was such that she no longer felt the ache in her thighs, that she no longer felt the bite of the wind on her face. She was now sure, more than she had ever been, that she would find Jack, that the universe wouldn't have put Brian in her path unless good things were supposed to happen.

She was two or three blocks south of the Bay Horse when she stopped for a traffic light. Looking around, she saw nothing. No traffic. She had the streets to herself and felt ridiculous for having stopped at all, but when she stepped into the street against the light, two things happened. The first was the thunk-thunk sound of anti-lock brakes coming at her from her left. The second was the sensation of being tugged backward, off the street and onto the sidewalk by the collar of her coat. Once Aria was standing on her own again, off the street, the driver took his foot off the brakes and allowed his vehicle to pass.

"You okay, Miss? Sorry I pulled so hard. I just didn't want you to get hit. That guy didn't have his lights on."

Aria turned to find herself facing a quasi-middle-aged gentlemen. His appearance indicated he was not new to life on the streets. She had no idea how she missed him, and the car, when she approached the corner.

"Oh, my God! Thank you so much. You saved my life."

The man chuckled.

"Well, I doubt that, but you're welcome. I figure there's not many people out tonight and we need everybody we can get."

Aria took a step forward and wrapped her arms around him, tears in her eyes, just as she had minutes before with Brian.

I must have a guardian angel, she thought.

The man returned the hug and chuckled again.

"Well, I have to say I'm having a good night. That's my second hug."

Aria released him.

"Do you need anything? Can I give you some money?"

She hated the fact that she asked the second question. Given the fact he had just saved her life, it sounded crass.

"Not tonight, Miss. Besides the hugs, a gentleman just gave me all the money he had in his pocket. I'm good. You just be careful!"

Aria turned to walk away, but something her guardian angel stopped her.

"Wait, someone gave you all their money? Do you mind me asking how long ago that happened?

"I don't mind. It was probably just ten or fifteen minutes ago."

Aria's heart pounded.

"Can you describe him?"

"Young guy, not much older than you, I think. He was tall. He was wearing a blue coat and a knit cap."

Jack!

Aria hugged him again.

"Thank you. Thank you. Thank you. Goodluck tonight."

"Well, well. Three hugs."

Mark E. Scott

The Roebling suspension bridge, spanning the Ohio River between Cincinnati and Covington, happened to have been designed by the same man who would go on to design the Brooklyn Bridge, a fact the tour guide failed to mention to Jack's tourist group the last time he was in Manhattan.

The Roebling was completely lit up as he approached it. As an engineer, he was able to appreciate the bridge on a number of levels, and again noted its beauty as the snow swirled around the cable towers. A park ran along the river and beneath the bridge. Jack could have taken the stairway up to the bridge from the park but chose instead to get there from the street above. The walkway, though covered in a non-slip material, was now slippery, and Jack was forced to grip the handrail in order to remain vertical as he made his way to the north tower.

The irony of trying *not* to fall was not lost on him. He just didn't want to go over the rail until he was over the water and had made his last entry.

Jack stopped walking when he reached the leeward side of the tower. On that side, he was protected from the wind and snow. He examined the sandstone and mortar around him, looking for a hole into which he could fit the notebook before he jumped. It didn't take him long to find one. While the bridge was kept in good shape, it was still more than 150 years old. There were bound to be chinks

Jack took the log out of his pocket and sat down with his back against the tower. Riffling through the pages, he was disappointed he had not filled every page. He let that disappointment go. There was nothing he could do about it now.

11:57
Well, this is about it, Posterity. These are my last words.

200

*I'm sitting on the bridge, writing this in the middle of a snow-
storm, so excuse the splotches.*
Just so you know, I didn't get here easily.
I understand why half my family stopped talking to me.
I might have done the same if I was one of them.
*In the end, it really just came down to two choices: live forever
with the pain and guilt*
of what I did to Troy or find a way to end it.
*As of now I have not been able to find a way to live with it, or
else I wouldn't be here.*
It all became too heavy. Too much.
Sometimes, I still feel his little body pressed against mine.
*Sometimes, I'm right back in the car with him, trapped, help-
less, and he's there, and he's dead. God help me, why did I live
and he died?*
If I could, I would go back and change things.
I would change things.
God help me.

"Jack!"

Aria had actually found him. She could hardly believe it. He was sitting on the bridge. He was still alive.

At first, Jack didn't believe what he was hearing. He thought it was
the wind or just his imagination

"Jack!"

Can't he hear me?

The wind may have been blocking Aria's voice.

No, he really heard it that time.

He closed the log, stood up, and, without thinking, slid it back in his
pocket. He couldn't believe what he was seeing and had forgotten about

stowing it in the mortar. Jack watched as Aria picked her way across the snowy walkway.

"Aria, what the hell are you doing here?!"

"I'm following you, Jack. I've been trying to catch up to you all night!"

She was nearly a hundred feet away, so yelling was required to be heard in the din of the storm. She inched forward.

"I read part of your log when you were in the bar, at Liberty's! I know what you're thinking about doing!"

Jack was stunned. *Was this really happening? Was it possible that Aria had really been searching for him all night?*

"Aria, please go. I'm fine."

He didn't know what else to say.

"You're not fine, Jack."

She was now only thirty or forty feet from him but had stopped moving. She wasn't holding the handrail anymore. She still felt lighter than air.

"I know, Jack, I know what you're feeling. Please let me help you. I can help you."

"Aria, please go. I decided to do this months ago. Please go. It's all too much."

Aria was walking and talking.

"It doesn't have to be, Jack. There are people who care about you . . . I care about you. I'm here for you, if you'll let me be."

"Why, Aria?"

Jack's voice weakened. He was overwhelmed. She was overwhelming. She looked beautiful, the snow swirling around her.

"I don't know exactly, Jack. But I'm here. Maybe it was the kiss. Maybe it's just because you're a . . ."

This was Aria's third fall of the evening. She had taken another step toward Jack, her hand reaching out to take his hand, when she hit a patch of ice. Now out of control, she slid sideways, and fell backward over the handrail.

Aria felt herself go over the rail. She felt herself falling. She made no sound because she couldn't believe she was actually falling into the river, at least not until she hit the water.

Jack stared into empty space, space that, until a fraction of a second ago, had been occupied by Aria., not sure he had seen what he had just seen. Aria was gone.

Jack stood and, without thinking, jumped over the rail right after Aria, hitting the water seconds later and nearly falling right on top of her.

The water was cold, not freezing but cold, and it worked its way through their clothing, numbing their skin and weighing them down. They roiled with the current, shocked and disoriented, struggling to regain control. Their bodies churned and swirled, connected with one another, drifting away for a moment only to join each other under the water again and again. Each knew the other was there, reached out for one another, but their hands would touch only long enough to confirm each of the other's existence, never long enough to get a grip.

Their clothes, now completely waterlogged, pulled them deeper beneath the surface. Neither knew any longer which way was up or down.

Under the water, desperation and disbelief, lungs burning, fighting the instinct to breathe, in a few moments they would have to give up.

They hit something.

That something was a coal barge, moored on the Ohio side of the river, waiting to be hauled upstream. They crashed into it simultaneously and, realizing they were no longer moving, desperately scrambled to crawl up the steel skin of the barge and onto the bank of the river.

Aria emerged first, with Jack close behind.

Jack didn't know it, but the Drunk Log was already a hundred yards down river. It had flown out of his back pocket as soon as he hit the water, out of reach before his head broke the surface.

The notebook would make its way down to Louisville and get stranded on the riverbank, close to the headquarters of the Louisville Slugger Bat Company. The following spring, a local high school student, who had volunteered for a river clean up, would find it and place it in a garbage bag, along with the other trash he had collected that day.

Aria and Jack paused, gave themselves a chance to breathe. Still in shock from their unexpected swimming expedition, neither of them had yet said a word.

They knew it was dangerous to stay where they were, and Aria managed to scramble out of the water first. When they could, they planted their feet and again reached for one another, each using the other as an anchor, something to help drag themselves out of the water.

"Take my hand."

About the Author

Mark E. Scott lives in downtown Cincinnati. In various work iterations he has, in no particular order, served in the U.S. Navy, flipped steaks at a chain restaurant, waited tables, repossessed cars, and delivered boat propellers to boat shops. For reasons not always clear, along the way Mark tried his hand at full-contact Kung Fu fighting, a sport at which he was mediocre at best. More productively, he also managed to obtain undergrad and graduate degrees in secondary education and business, respectively, the latter being the most useful of the two.

Coming Soon!

FIRST DATE
A DAY IN THE LIFE SERIES
BOOK 2
BY
MARK E. SCOTT

If you wanted a date so bad, all you had to do was ask...

First Date, Jack and Aria crash into the freezing cold river, seemingly by accident... They're deeply attracted to each other, but frozen, bruised and bleeding.

Will they surrender to their feelings for each other or continue protecting themselves in a haze of booze, drugs, and excuses? Can they save each other? Can each of them accept the gift they've been given...

This dark comedy builds on the themes of *Drunk Log*, Book One, the continuation of *A Day in the Life:* It confronts what happens to these two star-crossed dreamers, consumed by grief and remorse, searching for love and redemption.

For more information
visit: www.SpeakingVolumes.us

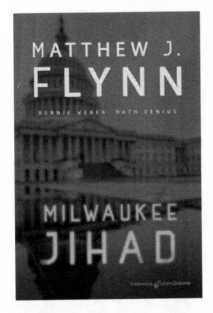

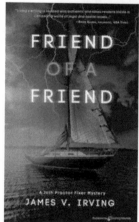
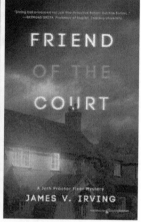

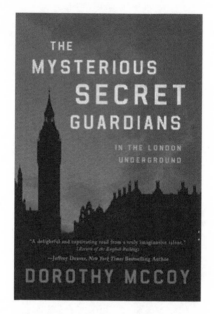

Made in the USA
Middletown, DE
01 November 2023

41780577R00130